DARK HORSES

The Magazine of Weird Fiction

MAY | 2022

No. 4

CONTENTS

THE RAISING OF
HESTER MACRAE

E.M. Anderson

"Hester knows, the moment she sets foot in the marketplace, that it will be a bad day. She keeps an ear open as she picks her way between market stalls, haggling less than usual over the price of salt, skeins of wool, the small, sweet oranges Annie loves so much. The morning is cold and slushy with the last of the latest snowfall. The old stone buildings lining either side of the street are crooked—the whole town is crooked, narrow, every building leaning in as if to hear whatever gossip is going around now—but today they seem more crooked than usual, looming over the marketplace until they threaten to suffocate it.

The whispers are everywhere.

"He was dead, I tell you."

"That's what I heard."

Hester listens as she slips through the market. She takes the small, soft steps that make everyone think her a gentlewoman but mostly ensure she'll draw as little notice as possible. Her stomach is clenched, her elbows close to her sides, her basket pressed tight to her stomach like a shield.

She's had decades of practice walking this way.

"Fell clean off the roof and snapped his neck."

"His mam was near screaming when she went running for the doctor."

"Well, he ain't dead now."

Only old Angus, the butcher, isn't suspicious.

"Mayhap the boy should've died," he says evenly to a knot of gossips, splitting a marrow bone for Hester's dog with his cleaver. "But he's a wee one. I've not heard his mam and pa gripe about his being alive. Can't ye call it a miracle and leave be?"

The shriveled woman who's in line behind Hester, even older than her and Annie, clicks her tongue. "Work o' the devil, more like. Only one word for it. Necromancy."

The gossips shift uneasily. No one knows for sure but Hester—not even Annie. But they all suspect, and that's all it takes.

"D'you reckon it was *her?*" a fresh-faced young housewife asks.

Annie, the housewife means. It wasn't Annie, of course. But Hester learned years ago that whenever anyone says *her* in that tone, they mean Annie.

Angus thuds his cleaver pointedly into his block and cracks the marrow bone apart with his hands. The gossips jump.

"*Her* wife is one o' my best customers," he says, in that same even tone. "So, I'll ask ye to take your blithering elsewhere."

Hester's fingers tighten on the handle of her basket as the gossips glance at her, but she allows a cold, polite smile to cross her face. Angus asks, "Just the one today?" and Hester nods, staring the gossips down until they look away, mumbling what may be apologies. The young woman blushes prettily and hurries on to the next stall.

Hester doesn't like having attention drawn to herself. Never has. It's safer not to be noticed.

But she knows the only reason her neighbors still tolerate Annie is because of her: because of the quiet old healer with her well-bred looks and pretty manners, and weren't they lucky she'd settled in their tiny town this decade past, and wasn't it a shame such a nice lady had taken up with *her?*

For Annie's sake, she'll risk notice.

For Annie's sake, she'll risk anything.

Almost.

Most of the gossips move off, but the shriveled old woman meets Hester's gaze and clicks her tongue again. Her eyes are milky with cataracts, but they're fearless, too.

"They mean no offense," she says, "but ye understand 'em. She's a witch, right enough. If ye weren't so damn fool in love with her, ye'd see it yourself."

Hester has seen it. She's seen Annie at her worst—and Annie's powers at their worst, too.

Hester stands ramrod straight, taking pleasure in all the height she has on this woman, well more than a foot.

"If that were true," she says coolly, "I should think you'd all be happy to see her using her powers this way. The McGuinty boy's only six years old."

The woman shakes her head. "T'ain't natural. T'ain't right. What's dead should stay dead."

Hester's skin prickles. She pays Angus without comment. As she places the marrow bone in her basket, she tells the woman, "I can take care of those cataracts for you, if you'd like. But you'll have to come by the shop."

The woman snorts. "Thank ye, no. I'd sooner go blind."

Hester sucks in her cheeks and moves off, clutching her basket tight. The gossip seeps from every corner of the marketplace like a mold infecting everything in its path.

"Never took her for a necromancer."

"Wouldn't put it past her."

"She's a witch—"

"—a monster—"

Hester leaves the market without her yarn as soon as she's bought Annie's oranges. For as long as she's in view of the marketplace, she keeps her steps slow and genteel, though her heart hammers, her skin prickles, and her legs itch to run, run. The moment she slips into the zigzagging alleyway at the market's edge, she hikes up her skirts and sprints. Old snow drips gray and cold from the roofs of the houses pressing in on either side.

The basket bounces painfully on her hip. Her heart is in her throat. The houses crowd the alleyway until she can't breathe.

Maybe it'll be fine. Annie hasn't had a bad day in years.

But if any of the gossips get to the shop before Hester—if Annie loses control and Hester isn't there—

Hester skids out onto the next street and collapses against the side of a house, sucking down air. She wants to throw up. Her lungs squeeze, her legs ache, a stitch stabs at her side, and all she can think of, suddenly, is the day she found Annie sprawled in the woods with a bullet in her neck.

Hester lets out a sob and presses a hand to her mouth. She leans her forehead to the cool stones of the house, trying to breathe, trying to swallow, trying not to cry.

The sick feeling passes. Hester hurries on. This time, she doesn't stop until she reaches home.

It's a two-story building where the town meets the outlying forest, the last human dwelling before miles of wilderness. Their apartment is above, Annie's florist shop below, with a small room in back where Hester sees patients when she's not making house calls. It's narrow, stone, and crooked, like every other building in town.

Unlike every other building in town, it's overgrown with plants—green even in January—and patched with mortar from all the times they've punched through its walls.

A small crowd gathers at the bottom of the stoop. Several of the gossips from the marketplace, their husbands, and grown-up sons. A roundsman in helmet and uniform. A farmer, name of Amos. Hester nursed his granddaughter through whooping cough earlier this winter.

Every man among them has a hunting rifle or shotgun in his hands, even Amos. There's a club in the roundsman's belt, too, and Hester's lived here long enough to suspect more than one in the crowd has a knife tucked into belt or boot. They weren't armed, last time they came around.

Hester dabs her brow with a handkerchief, smooths her hair and skirts. Arranges her face into an expression of polite bemusement. She holds her basket at her side, draws herself up to her full height—taller than most of them, though she's skilled at shrinking herself to avoid notice—and crosses the street with the same slow, genteel steps she took in the marketplace.

"So many visitors," she says, in a voice that's quiet but carries, nonetheless. The crowd turns. One of the gossips flushes, pressing close to her husband. The young housewife from the market. "We appreciate the business, to be sure. But I fear I must remind you all that the shop is closed on Saturdays."

The gossips and their families have the grace to look ashamed of themselves. Amos scuffs the ground with his boot. The roundsman looks bullish.

The crowd parts reluctantly as Hester steps into their midst, moving steadily toward the shop. Her voice is calm, but her heart races. The stoop seems so far away, the arms so close.

"I will of course be happy to see any of you at home," she says, "if it's healing you have need of."

"Don't none of us need anything," the roundsman says easily, "but to see that witch run out o' town. S'been a long time coming."

Hester's knuckles whiten on her basket. "Then it'll keep."

A husband shakes his head. "Not anymore, it won't. The McGuinty boy's the last straw."

Hester flinches. Her fault.

Everyone murmurs in agreement.

"What's dead should stay dead," Amos says.

If Hester believed that, Annie would be dead of a gunshot wound years ago, and Hester would be alone in the world. Her skin prickles, face and neck and chest and arms. The murmurs rise and sharpen around her until they buzz inside her like a swarm of hornets. She keeps walking, but the stoop doesn't get any closer, they've stopped parting to let her through, they crowd around her with that same suffocating force as the buildings at the market and the houses along the alleyway, and then the front door bangs open, and Annie is there with the dog at her side.

Hester's heart skips a beat. Annie's hair hangs in one long, silver rope over her shoulder. Her arms are corded with muscle. An apron is tied over her skirts, dusted heavily with flour. Saturday is her baking day.

The crowd draws closer together. The roundsman fingers his club, the others their guns. The dog, Hamish, presses against Annie's legs with a whine.

Hester holds her basket so tight against her that it digs into her stomach.

Annie's eyes flicker over the crowd, snagging on Hester before they move on. Long enough for Hester to see the fear in them. Not for herself: Annie has long resigned herself to one day being run off or killed by the folks she grew up with. There was no surprise over the bullet in her neck all those years ago, only surprise that she'd survived it.

No. Annie's scared for Hester, caught down there between their neighbors.

However much they mutter, Hester heals their ills and injuries, cares for their children when there's no one else and they must be gone, speaks softly and smiles quietly and never bothers anyone or causes any trouble. As far as the town is concerned, Hester is a sweet old newcomer who had the misfortune to fall under the witch's spell.

But as scared as Annie is, she's not scared enough. If the town knew the truth, they'd fear Hester even more than they fear her wife.

"What's going on here?" Annie growls, crossing her arms.

"We got business with you," the roundsman says, thumbing up the brim of his helmet.

Annie's arms tighten across her chest. Flowers sprout at her heels, heedless of the cold: monkshood, petunias, poisonously orange lilies. Danger. Anger. Hatred.

"We're closed. Shove off and leave your business 'til Monday. Come on inside, Hettie, there's lunch."

But the crowd hems Hester in, and she cannot come on inside. Cyclamen sprouts at Annie's feet.

Whatever happens, Hester tells herself, it will be all right. Whatever happens, she can fix it. She struggles to breathe with the warmth of her neighbors' bodies pressed so close, but she keeps repeating it to herself. *Whatever happens. Whatever happens. Whatever happens.*

A rose vine with black blooms snakes up the doorframe. Hamish skitters away from it, his claws clicking on the floor, and darts inside with his tail between his legs.

The roundsman's eyes follow the path of those black roses. "It can't wait. The McGuinty boy—"

Annie shrinks in on herself. Hester opens her mouth to say something, anything. To tell them it wasn't Annie. To tell them it was her. Nothing comes out.

"That weren't me," Annie says in a quivering voice. Hester's heart twists. Annie would never let them think Hester had done it if the situation were reversed. But Hester's voice is caught deep inside her, so used to silence it's all but choked out. "I never laid eyes on that boy."

"That's a lie." The young housewife, red-cheeked and frightened and determined. "He were in here with his mam not two days afore he fell off that roof."

Hester remembers. She gave him a peppermint while his mother tried and failed to talk Annie down on the price of two arrangements of woodland flowers.

"I didn't," Annie says. Foxglove and butterfly weed bloom violently around her, splintering the door. The gossips flinch. A husband raises his rifle. "I didn't, I never—ye know me—the plants, it's all I do, ye must know that—"

"Annie," Hester whispers. Annie can't hear her, but Hester knows this voice, knows Annie's trying to keep herself in check. Somewhere inside the shop, glass shatters as flowers burst into being, smashing the vases by the register, and Hamish yelps from wherever he's hiding, and Hester wishes she had power that could help Annie from here. Any kind of power other than the one she has.

"If'n ye leave now," Amos says, not unkindly, "there won't be no trouble."

"No," Hester croaks.

"Ye can stay, Miss Hester," Amos says. "We'd be sorry to lose ye. But ye can't keep your wife and your house both."

"Leave her out of this," Annie snaps.

"All due respect," a gossip says, not sounding respectful at all, "but it was you what brung her into it when ye married her."

"Annie," Hester repeats, louder, because tansies are shooting up tall and yellow around the stoop now, encroaching on the garden and the walkway and the crowd at the bottom of the steps, and Annie's nostrils are flaring and she doesn't even notice all the flowers now, Hester can tell, and it's only a matter of time until—

The roundsman grabs Hester's elbow, yanks her toward him. She stumbles. Oranges fall from her basket and roll away.

"If'n you won't leave on our say-so, maybe you'll leave for her." His fingers are vicelike on Hester's arm. Her throat is dry. "Ye clear out right now," he says, "and I'll leave her go. If'n ye don't—"

"Bern," Amos says uncomfortably. "Bern, I don't think—"

"Don't none of you think. Ye want her gone? This'll get her gone."

The others exchange uneasy glances. No one's quarrel is with Hester.

But no one else says anything.

The roundsman's fingers tighten on Hester's elbow. "Your choice, witch."

Annie's voice is deadly quiet. "Leave her go."

"Clear out, and I will."

"Annie," Hester says, but Annie ignores her.

"Let go of her first."

"Please," Hester says to the roundsman, but he shakes her into silence.

"Make me," he says.

Annie's eyes flash. *Let go of her!*

As if sucked in by the house inhaling deeply, the plants in the doorway crowd around her.

Then they explode.

Stalks and leaves punch through the walls, showering the crowd with rubble. The gossips shriek, banging into each other in their haste to escape. The husbands raise their rifles but don't fire, unsure whether they should aim at Annie or the plants or the falling chunks of stone. Amos fumbles with his shotgun but stumbles back from the stoop without using it. Hamish barks inside the house.

And still the plants come. The ground shakes and rumbles as tree trunks shoot up through the street. Vines whip out from the shop to snake around ankles, legs, waists. The young housewife screams as a vine drags her husband to the ground.

"Remain calm!" the roundsman shouts, sounding anything but calm himself.

Hester stamps on his foot, rams him in the stomach with her basket, and sprints for the door.

A gunshot cracks in her ear. She drops into a crouch, breathing hard.

"Annie!" she cries, but Annie's there in the doorway, eyes aglow, braid whipping around her as plants splinter floorboards and smash stones and shatter glass. Somewhere inside, Hamish's barking reaches fever pitch, turns into a yelp, then a whimper, then breaks off.

Another gunshot, and a bullet ricochets off the doorframe. Trees close in on the garden, blocking the street and the crowd from view. They creak and groan as they grow lightning-fast to shield the house. Outside their protective circle, the screams of the crowd are muffled. Bullets thud into bark and then die away. Branches interlock overhead until the stoop is in shadow.

Hester rises slowly and limps up the steps, her breathing harsh and loud in her ears. Annie stares straight ahead, lost somewhere in her anger and her fear and her magic.

It's not the first time. But Hester's never seen it this bad.

"Annie," she says softly. "Annie, it's all right."

Annie turns toward her, expression blank. Hester sets her basket on the stoop and steps closer. Her heart rabbits against her ribcage. No matter how many times it happens, it never scares her less: not the explosive plants, or the holes in the walls, but Annie blank and glowing, lost somewhere where Hester can't be sure of finding her. Annie afterward, shame-faced and shrunken and scared of it happening again. Calling herself a witch and a monster like their neighbors do.

"Annie," Hester whispers. "They're gone. I'm right here. Everything's all right."

Everything except that they'll have to move on. Hester's throat constricts at the thought of leaving their shop behind, and the garden, and the cow in the shed out back. She blinks the feeling away. It won't be the first time she's packed up her life. At least this time she won't be alone.

She touches Annie's cheek. Annie's expression doesn't change, but she shudders.

Hester presses her forehead to Annie's, cupping her wife's face in her hands. The earth shakes around them, but Hester breathes in Annie's scent, fresh bread and dirt and black tea, and strokes the sides of her face, and whispers over and over, "I'm right here."

At last, the world goes quiet. The plants quiver, then still. Annie heaves in a breath, the glow in her eyes fading.

"Hester?" she says in a small voice.

Hester lets out a shaky breath and kisses her forehead. "Right here, darling."

Annie pulls away and slumps against the wall, passing a hand over her eyes. Her shoulders shake. A low sob escapes her.

Hester touches her back.

"It's not as bad as all that," she says, but Annie shrugs her off, and her words ring hollow in her own ears.

It shouldn't have happened like this. If she'd only told them it was her, not Annie. If she'd left the McGuinty boy alone. If she'd kept her promise to herself, the same promise she makes every time she starts over: not to use her gift.

The same promise she breaks, no matter where she goes, no matter how many times she tells herself it'll be different now.

Annie plods down the hall, picking things up at random and tucking them into the crook of one arm. A portrait of the two of them that fell off the wall. The set of keys that shook right off the hook by the door. A book with pages pulled loose by the commotion. The plants bend toward her as she goes, stretching to brush against her comfortingly with their leaves.

"M'sure Angus'll fix it up nice for ye," Annie says hoarsely.

Hester trails after her. "What are you talking about?"

"Ye should stay, Hettie." Annie's shoulders are hunched. "They like ye well enough. Ye could stay."

Hester's face prickles hot with shame, but she catches one of Annie's hands in her own. "Not without you."

Annie moans. Hamish lies dead on the splintered floor, tangled in vines. Portrait, keys, book, everything in Annie's arms clatters to the ground. She drops to her knees at the dog's side, reaches out as if to stroke his fur. Her fingers curl in at the last moment like she's afraid to touch him. As if she could hurt him now.

Hester kneels at her side.

"Oh, Hamish," she murmurs. "Sweet boy."

Her eyes sting, but she's not one to let a little thing like death get in her way.

It's time Annie knew anyway.

Hester untangles the dog gently. Annie's jaw tightens.

"Ye see?" she whispers. "Ye'd be better off without me."

Hester's heart clenches. She turns toward Annie and kisses her hands fervently. Annie's cheeks are wet.

"I'm not staying here without you," Hester says. "Nor anywhere else."

"Ye could have a life."

Hester cups her wife's face in her hands and kisses her, slow and gentle. Annie's breath hitches. She touches Hester's neck tentatively, her fingers barely there, then slides her hand around to tangle in Hester's long tresses and kisses her back. They press their foreheads together, breathing the same air.

"It's no life without you," Hester says. "I love you, Annie Macrae."

Annie's fingers tighten in her hair. "Even though I'm a monster."

Something cavernlike opens in Hester's chest. She kisses Annie again, once, softly.

"I love you because you're a monster," she says.

Annie sniffles. Then she says, "That's the daftest thing ye've ever said."

Hester chuckles wetly, kisses her forehead, and returns to disentangling Hamish from plant matter. Annie will understand once she knows.

Annie watches her work, brow drawn.

"Leave him," she says wearily. "It won't make no difference."

Hester rubs the pads of Hamish's paws as she slides vines over his front legs. He always liked it when she rubbed his paw pads. "It'll make some difference."

Annie wipes her eyes on her apron.

"Why?" she asks. "Ye could've had anyone. Why the monster?"

Hester doesn't answer. Instead, she frees Hamish from the last of the vines. She cradles him to her as she did the McGuinty boy only days ago, letting his frailty and mortality flood her lungs, ribs, heart, and stomach: always the worst part of the process. It's suffocating, like some creeping vine is growing over her innards and choking out her own life.

"Hettie," Annie says, "what are ye doing? He's gone."

The suffocating feeling fades. Hester breathes deeply, then traces a triskelion over Hamish's heart. She breathes gently into his nose.

Waits.

His heart thuds. Once. Twice. Then continuously.

Hamish snorts, twisting in Hester's arms like he's awoken from a nap. Hester lets out a breath, the corner of her mouth turning up, and kisses his nose.

She risks a glance at Annie. Her skin prickles all over; she feels exposed. Flayed and bare like she's laid out on a dissecting table. She's never done this in front of anyone before. Not on purpose. Whenever she's caught, that's when she leaves.

Annie's brow is furrowed, but she runs a hand over Hamish's side. He yips and strains to lick her face. For once, she lets him.

"Hamish?" Her gaze slides over Hettie, uncertain but not fearful, not angry. "Hettie—what—?"

Hester gives a slight shrug. A small smile. When she takes Annie's hand, Annie doesn't pull away.

"I'm a monster, too," she says.

QUERY LETTER

Riley Winchester

L Bennett Hart
4917 Mondale Ave.
Apartment 6
Dorr, MI 49323

Beth Huttenbach, Editor
Chinle Books
305 Montague St.
Suite 200
Chinle, AZ 86503

Dear Beth,

Though we didn't speak much more than a few words, I met you at AWP a few years ago. Forgive me for not being able to recollect the exact year—I've been to a handful—and you must understand the circumstances I'm in right now. Since that nondescript meeting, I've had various stories and essays published in journals. No books yet, but I think this one may be of interest to you. Sorry it took me so long to type those sentences. What am I saying? You won't even know how long it took me to write this paragraph. I shouldn't have apologized. Forget about that. I'd delete it, but I'm afraid I'm short on time. Oh dear, I'm more nervous than I thought. But you must understand. This is terrifying and I've never done anything like it before.

AMERICAN SUBLIME is the story of an American midwestern family's coming together and undoing. There's love, illness, unexpected joys, and unavoidable miseries. It's mostly about the vagaries of life, how much it fuckin sucks—especially as I write this. You can do everything right and then one day something or somebody will knock on your door (or break it down, in this case) and your entire equilibrium and equanimity will go up in flames in a frankly pathetic display. But back to the book. Think *They Came Like Swallows,* by William Maxwell meets, oh, I don't know, *East of Eden,* by John Steinbeck? I don't know. I never prepped this far in my query letter and I'm only looking at the books on the shelf next to my desk (he won't let me get up and look at the rest of the library).

You know what? Time to quit being so coy. He won't let me think for one damn second as I write this. I said I needed to go to my bookshelf to find some comparisons and he said no I had to stay seated and write my last words. I guess I'm grateful in a way. It's not every day that a murderous psychopath breaks into your apartment to kill you and has the magnanimity to grant you your last words. He's going to kill me, there's no doubt about that, but he said I can send one last thing out. Figured it's a fair trade.

And here's the thing, Beth, I kind of panicked when I chose you to be the recipient of my last words. I've been writing this book for a while now and all my friends and family have laughed at my aspirations of being a writer and I've read some of the books your house has published and, well, I think everything came together in a beautiful little shitstorm and here we are. I'm a failure. A soon to be murdered failure. And now I've dragged you into this, Beth. Truth be told, the book is ROUGH. The bones are there, sure, but it isn't ready. Do you think this will be an issue? Can you fix it? You and Chinle Books are my last hope.

Good god. He's such a cliché too. Nice enough to let me haphazardly knock this letter out but he keeps destroying my shit. Smashed my futon and TV; he's ripping up books; he's throwing food away; he just tried to flush a cardigan down the toilet. Oh no, did referring to my possessions as *shit* earlier in this paragraph evince their superfluity to me? Beth, this is not the time for an existential crisis. God, I've always abhorred that phrase. I hate my possessions; I hate my words. Beth, what is there to like about me? I'm a sad sack of soon-to-be-dead flesh. And all he brought was a KNIFE. I'm about to be chopped up like it's the Crusades or something. At least put a bullet in my head like a modern murderer.

But I'm getting off-track. The book is good stuff, really. You'll have to rework a lot before it's ready to publish, but I give you full permission to do it. I trust you. I've read Chinle Books. OK, confession: I've read like thirty pages of one book and a few of another. BUT I liked them. And you were the first draft email to pop up. I had forty-seven drafts in my Gmail, all publishing houses. You weren't my first pick. There! I said it! You were just the one I clicked. Please publish my book. I panicked, OK. He said he'd let me send out my last words, and I always wanted to write a book. Did I say this earlier?

AMERICAN SUBLIME follows the DuBois family in rural Illinois. The matriarch, Paige DuBois, falls ill with leukemia and the family... oh fuck this. Just please read the manuscript. Beth, I'm about to be murdered. Murdered by a stupid knife. You should see this thing. People in this country are worried about the guns, but nobody talks knives.

OH MY GOD.

He put my iPad in the air fryer.

Shit, he caught me looking. He's coming over here. Jesus, that frying iPad already smells terrible. This is what the cops will smell when they find me? This keeps getting more pathetic. *I* keep getting more pathetic.

He looks pissed; this stabbing is going to hurt extra hard. When I sign my name here soon I'm going to instantly hit send so please excuse any errors or digressions. AMERICAN SUBLIME, think about it, Beth. Oh, sweet tap-dancing Christ, I forgot to ATTACH it. Hold on, I hope he doesn't think I'm doing anything funny.

OK, good. Got it attached. So here it is, Beth.

Fuck. There *it* is. Who picks the first stab site to be the shoulder blade? Ah, fuckingoddamnshitsonofabitch this hurts. I'm typing with one hand now. Well, he seems determined to finish what he started (good lesson for us writers), so I must sign off now.

The manuscript is almost complete at 111,000 words or something. Work your magic, Beth.

I'm really losing a lot of blood here.

Tallyho,

Bennett Ha

OCTOBER MARDI GRAS

Mary Joe Rabe

It started snowing around noon two days before Halloween, and the temperature sank respectively. Completely unaffected by the weather, the high school band marched enthusiastically up and down the football field, the kids proudly carrying their instruments. Marching went well; playing while marching, not as well, but the kids were having a good time. They wouldn't embarrass themselves in the parade.

Daniel Audelheim stood on the crumbling sidewalk at the corner of Section Road and Wilson Street and watched and listened intently. He was freezing and wished he had bothered to bring along a cap and mittens. Grandma would probably say this is what he got from being so skinny, no layer of fat beneath the skin to protect him from the cold.

The traffic on Section Road, as usual, was minimal, just the occasional plodding tractor. He shivered — he'd been doing that a lot lately — but the pleasant scent of not yet harvested corn wafted over the football field and cheered him up.

This was the best part of his job, the interaction with the kids. Sure, some of them were better musicians than others, but they had all improved since he started teaching band and vocal music here in Tetes des Morts at the end of August. And they all liked playing in the band. They were good kids, mostly hard-working farm kids for whom school activities were the high point of their days.

Not all the parents were in favor of having their property tax pay for high school band. Fortunately, the state of Iowa forced high schools to offer instruction in vocal and instrumental music. So, it was just a matter of getting to the kids before their parents could talk them out of it. He had been able to persuade a number of junior high kids to start playing a musical instrument, using up all the instruments the school had on hand to rent out to kids.

He needed more instruments that the kids could rent instead of buying, just like he needed more funds to buy sheet music, both for instrumental and vocal music. He certainly needed better music room facilities. Those were some of the disadvantages of this job.

The worst part of the job, however, concerned a few of his teacher colleagues. As far as he could tell, they were as mean to him as they were to their poor students.

"By the way, why do the people here celebrate Halloween by calling it Mardi Gras?" Daniel asked one of the few friendly teachers later that afternoon. He squirmed in his uncomfortable folding chair and stretched his long legs out in front of him.

The lengthy, but narrow room was furnished haphazardly with an indifferent interior design. Armless, cushioned chairs of varying colors, shapes, and aged upholstery lined up along two walls. Flimsy folding chairs and two dilapidated couches, one green and one brown, stood under each window. Each wall was painted a different shade of orange. Cheap copies of various paintings hung on the walls, dogs playing cards, fields of impressionist flowers.

It was the last Tuesday in October 1968. He still didn't feel like he belonged in this depressing, smoke-filled teachers' lounge in

Tetes des Morts, Iowa, a town settled a hundred years ago by Luxembourg emigrants.

No one knew anymore why they gave it this name. It was a typical, small farming town in Iowa with a population of about five hundred people and city limits that stretched out around an area of about one and a quarter square miles, or eight hundred acres.

The school campus — grade school, junior high, and high school, all imposing brick buildings from the 1950's — was located at the east end of town. The cemetery bordered to the north, with corn fields on the farms to the east and south.

The townspeople, as to be expected in Iowa, were extremely hospitable. The town had even set up a trailer park up the hill from the cemetery for the many teachers who came to Tetes des Morts and stayed one or two years while they looked for better-paying jobs. Teachers with access to more money generally bought houses in Tetes des Morts.

Daniel lived in the trailer park, more or less to his satisfaction. The single-wide trailer he rented had everything he needed, and the town took care of the grounds.

He couldn't complain about his living conditions except for the nightmares he had ever since he moved in. They were probably due to the stress from some of his unpleasant colleagues. On the other hand, he had never had nightmares before, not even during nerve-racking experiences with his rock and roll band or during dealings with their viciously criminal record company.

Daniel had exchanged his shoulder-length, brown, curly hair for a crew cut that left determining the hair color up to the observer. Instead of his torn blue jeans and tie-dye t-shirts he wore uncomfortable suits and ties. At twenty-two he wasn't that much older than the high school students he was supposed to teach music to, but he now looked and felt like he belonged to their grandparents' generation.

It was 1968 in the rest of the world, but in Tetes des Morts, it might as well be 1958. Ever since his interview the past spring, Daniel had wondered if he could transition from college-student drummer in a rock and roll band to school band leader in a very conservative farm community.

Circumstances made the decision fairly easy. After his college band disintegrated due to differing opinions regarding the direction it should take, he and the other members were left with debts to the record company in addition to their student loans.

He needed a job, and the Tetes des Morts high school didn't demand a teaching certificate. When he took the job, he thought he could earn some easy money and finally have time for his own compositions. Later, he could go back to the music business.

Patricia Hammond, the friendly, young — though not nearly as young as he was — colleague sitting next to him shook her longish, blonde hair that bent up stiffly at her shoulders. "Why," she answered. "I have no idea why they call it Mardi Gras, and I'm married to a man whose family has been farming here for over a hundred years."

"The Mardi Gras parade organizers in the fine city of Benton would say that it has always been that way," Patricia continued. "In reality, they started the parade just twenty years ago in the hopes that it would keep potential teenage mischief-makers busy in positive, wholesome ways on Halloween."

"That's why there is a parade in Iowa on Halloween evening when it is usually bitterly cold?" Daniel asked. "You'd think the weather alone would keep marauding teenagers at home."

"It would be just as cold in February or March when everyone else celebrates Mardi Gras," Patricia said. "So, they might as well have their celebration now. Maybe someone saw the real Mardi Gras in New Orleans and thought it was just like Halloween, what with the costumes and all. Maybe they call their Halloween parade Mardi Gras to make it sound like something special."

"They do invite all the high school marching bands in the vicinity to participate. Your predecessors here all refused to let the kids take part, but it seems that you accepted the challenge without knowing what you were getting yourself into."

"I asked the kids at band practice, and they were all for it," Daniel said helplessly. "I'm new here. I didn't want the kids to hate me as much as my colleagues do."

"They don't all hate you,'" Patricia said. "You just got off on the wrong foot with Principal Jolly and his science teacher wife Suzette. They didn't like it when you complained about your working conditions and the lack of instruments and sheet music for the kids in your classes."

"And with Paul Palmer," Daniel said.

"When you criticized his choices for the junior and senior class plays and suggested that he consider doing musicals," Patricia said, rolling her eyes slightly. Daniel knew she meant well. Patricia was patient with everyone.

With that their conversation halted. The door to the hall opened, some of the thick cigarette smoke blew out, and the rest of the faculty dashed in and fought for chairs.

Principal Jolly, an older, portly, red-faced gentleman, waddled over to the center of the room. As usual he opened the meeting with a long harangue about how the school board demanded further savings.

"Does that mean I don't get a new band room?" Daniel asked sarcastically.

"We all have to make do," Principal Jolly barked.

"Music classes and band practice take place in an old wooden, one-room schoolhouse next to the parking lot," Daniel said. "These kids work hard and deserve better."

Principal Jolly ignored him. Suzette Jolly said, "We all have to make do," and smirked as she gazed at Paul Palmer. Mrs. Jolly's suspiciously jet-black hair was flawlessly coiffed, and she was dressed like an over-anxious sales representative with her navy jacket, white blouse, navy skirt, and patent-leather dark blue high heels.

She was well-known for intimidating and ridiculing her unfortunate science students. Daniel thought she was scary. She reminded him of some of the teachers who had bullied him back when he was in high school.

Paul Palmer, a tall, lanky, fiftyish man with unkempt, collar-length gray hair that fell into his eyes looked up and bellowed in a deep voice, "If you don't like it here, go teach somewhere else. Wait, you can't, can you? You don't even have a teaching certificate." As usual Mr. Palmer reeked of beer and slurred his words slightly.

Daniel was relieved when the teachers' conference was finally over. It had been the usual waste of time for all concerned.

He did come to one conclusion, though. The contract for the band's performance in the upcoming parade was between him as band leader and the Benton Mardi Gras organization.

Daniel decided that he would keep the money that the Mardi Gras parade paid for his band's performance and splurge on sheet music with it instead of handing it in to the principal's office. Suzette Jolly and Paul Palmer had said he should always just buy one set of sheet music for each piece and mimeograph off enough copies for the choirs, but he refused. Even if most of the money went to the publishing companies, he didn't want to cheat composers out of their royalties.

That night his nightmares were worse than usual. He was a student in a chemistry class where Suzette Jolly was berating a girl who started crying. Then he was in an English class where Paul Palmer threw a bust of Shakespeare at a boy who stuttered. The worst part of it was that he was paralyzed and couldn't come to the assistance of the poor kids. He was relieved to wake up.

Halloween Day was a cold and snowy Thursday. Tetes des Morts High School had never had a marching band before, but the kids had practiced every day for weeks for this opportunity. They continued to improve. They no longer ran into each other as much. They could even march and stay in their designated rows while playing.

They just wouldn't be able to do any of the fancy stuff like creating pictures, but that wasn't necessary. No one would be watching them from above like in a football stadium. All the spectators would be shivering on the sidewalks at the sides of the streets while the band went by.

It was getting cold even though it was only the sixth hour class. Daniel worried that the band uniforms wouldn't be warm enough that evening. They had been sewn by home ec classes over the years, made of cheap materials the teacher managed to scrounge around for. "Hey, kids," he shouted. "Stop marching and come over here." The kids ran across the field.

"We need to get our schedule down," Daniel said to the crowd of kids holding or standing next to their instruments. "First of all, it's getting cold, so wear as much warm clothing under your band uniforms as you can. Second, get here on time. The school bus will leave from Wilson Street, here in front of the high school, at six p.m. so that we get to Benton by six-thirty. Third, behave yourselves before, during, and after the parade. We want to make a good impression so that we get invited back."

"So," he continued. "You're dismissed. Leave your instruments in the band room and go to your seventh hour classes. I'll see you later this afternoon."

Daniel walked over to the school bus garage. He might not have a teaching certificate, but he had all kinds of driver's licenses, truck, chauffeur, etc. His time in the rock band had included working as a roadie, driving to gigs where they had to bring all their own equipment. So, he happily augmented his low teacher's salary by driving a school bus.

The kids came dashing out of the buildings shortly after three. Daniel had an easy route, a lot of paved stretches, little traffic on the gravel roads. The kids were rambunctious but not malicious. The older ones were often quite talkative.

"You driving to Benton tonight, Mr. Audelheim?" Brian Greeve, a perhaps lazy but good-natured sixteen-year-old, asked. As usual, Brian had no books with him. He hardly ever bothered doing work for school at home. He got his perfect attendance award each year and managed to maintain his C-minus grade-point average.

Daniel drove off slowly. "Yes," he answered. "The band is marching in the Mardi Gras parade in Benton tonight, and so it made sense for me to drive."

"You might want to take the longer highway route," Brian said. "The shorter route up and down the gravel-road hills won't have the snow cleared after eight p.m."

"Thanks," Daniel said. "Are you going to watch the parade?"

"Haven't decided," Brian said. "My parents are going. Is Mrs. Jolly going to accompany the band as a chaperone?"

"Yeah," Daniel said. "That surprised me. She is never that supportive of the band otherwise."

Brian laughed. "She and Palmer do that a lot," he said. "It's only a secret from Principal Jolly. Palmer will drive to Benton, go get drunk somewhere, and she'll join him at a motel while the band is marching. They do that for lots of activities that she supposedly chaperones."

"I didn't know that," Daniel said truthfully. "I could tell they were friends, but I thought that was because they both came here from Mittelwert High School five years ago."

"Everyone here also knows why they had to leave Mittelwert," Brian said. "Some kids there committed suicide because of how Mrs. Jolly and Mr. Palmer treated them in class. The school board wanted to fire them, but there was no proof of anything and they both had tenure. So, the town bribed them to leave. How do you think they could afford to buy the biggest houses in Tetes des Morts when they came here?"

"I had no idea," Daniel said as he gently brushed the brake to avoid running into a huge boar while not skidding the school bus off the snow-covered gravel road. "How do you know this stuff?"

"My dad's the chairman of the school board here, remember?" Brian said. "The board was glad to get both Jollys cheap, and Mr. Palmer had a state-wide reputation of being a great teacher except when he was sober. Dad said they figured us kids were strong enough to put up with a few mean teachers."

"And are you?" Daniel asked.

"Most of us are," Brian said. "But mean teachers always figure out which kids they can bully. We all wish the three of them would leave. My dad says they won't be satisfied with their low salaries here forever."

Daniel had a hard time processing this new information, but he finished his route and got all the kids home safely. He was back at his trailer by four-thirty and decided to lie down for an hour. Unfortunately, the nightmares started as soon as he closed his eyes. Translucent figures flew in the air up around his bed.

"We're not a nightmare," one of them said. "You are a good person, Daniel. Help us."

Daniel tried to open his eyes but felt paralyzed. "What do you want?" he tried to say, but maybe just thought.

The translucent figures transformed into traumatized faces of teenage boys and girls. "It's the time of year when spirits of those once living can seek justice," one of the girls said. "We are the victims from Mittelwert. The spirits from the cemetery here are loaning us their strength and power so that we can communicate with you."

"Okay," Daniel thought doubtfully.

"We need to bring those two cruel teachers to justice," a boy said. "That was denied to us in life. But we can deal with them once they are with us in death. There are many of us, and the spirit world allows eternal punishment for the truly evil."

"Why me and why now?" Daniel asked.

"We followed Mr. Palmer and Mrs. Jolly here. The spirits of Tetes des Morts offered us their help. Halloween is when the worlds of the living and the worlds of the dead converge for a few hours. You are the first person who listened when we cried," the girl said. "Please deliver Suzette Jolly and Paul Palmer to us tonight."

"How am I supposed to do that?" Daniel asked. "I can't kill people for you, even if I think the world would be better off without those two."

"Please," the girl said. Suddenly Daniel could move, could open his eyes. He shivered uncontrollably. His nightmares were definitely getting worse. He needed to eat something before he left for the bus garage. He needed to be in better shape before he drove the band to Benton.

Daniel's heartbeat and probably his blood pressure were back to normal by the time he was waiting at the bus. He had to help the kids stow the larger instrument cases in the back of the bus. Most of the kids had to hold their cases in their laps for the drive. When he walked back to the driver's seat, he heard how Suzette Jolly was ridiculing a girl.

"You'll need to get a different uniform," Suzette said to one of the shy freshman girls. "You are much too fat for this one."

"No," Daniel said to the girl who looked like she wanted to run and hide. "Mrs. Jolly is wrong. You look great."

Staring at Suzette Jolly he continued, "Mrs. Jolly, you are here as a chaperone, not as a fashion designer. I told the kids to wear as much clothing as possible under these thin uniforms. I don't want anyone catching pneumonia in this parade because they aren't dressed warmly enough."

Suzette, to her credit, looked surprised. "We'll discuss your impertinent tone of voice tomorrow, Mr. Audelheim," she said. "Non-tenured teachers are well-advised to show the tenured faculty more respect."

Ignoring her, Daniel said to the kids already on the bus, "And even if it is Halloween, no one needs to look like a scrawny bag of bones."

The kids laughed. Suzette looked shocked, but she took a seat in the front row and said nothing. Daniel guessed that she didn't want to miss her date with Paul Palmer.

He took the short but hilly route to Benton, assuming that it would still be quicker than taking the highway. The snow was getting thicker on the gravel road, but he got them to the riverside parking lot in Benton where the parade began on time. Suzette Jolly stomped off the bus and disappeared. Daniel helped the kids get their instruments out and ready to play. They got in formation and had to wait in line for their place in the parade.

Daniel took his position as band leader and as soon as the signal from the organizers came, the band moved into its position and started off marching. The kids' instruments gleefully blared out the Tetes des Morts fight song, followed by other old marches they didn't need to pay to play. The spectators on the sidewalks all cheered and clapped. It kept snowing as the temperatures continued to drop.

The parade ended two hours later back at the parking lot where the organizers handed out various trinkets of recognition. The Tetes des Morts high school band got a special ribbon as the crowd favorite of the parade. Coincidentally enough, the Benton high school band got a blue ribbon for top quality.

"Next year we'll get that blue ribbon, too," Daniel yelled to his band. "Go get yourselves something warm to eat and drink and be back at the bus in half an hour." The parking lot had all kinds of booths around its perimeter, guaranteed by the parade management to be alcohol free. The kids packed their instruments away, left the cases in the bus, and went off to get hot chocolate and cupcakes.

Daniel looked off into the sky. The clouds were shaping themselves into the translucent faces of his nightmares. "Help us," their mouths seemed to say.

Suzette sauntered up to the bus after the last kid had left. "There will be consequences," she slurred.

"You're drunk," Daniel said. "You don't want the kids to see you like this. Some of their teetotaling parents might mention your inadequate chaperone performance to the school board. You don't want to risk more complaints."

"I know you're here with Paul Palmer," he continued. "I can see his dented sports car over there. Ride back with him. I'm guessing he's as drunk as you are. So, make sure he follows me slowly and carefully. He won't lose sight of this huge, yellow school bus."

Suzette glared at him but stumbled over to the dented sports car. Daniel began to see the translucent faces more clearly. He felt empowered. He was no longer the helpless kid in a high school class; he was the conduit for powers beyond his knowledge and control.

He had time to put chains on the tires. They would get the bus through any weather conditions.

The kids all came back to the bus, and Daniel drove off confidently, though slowly, taking the snowy, hilly route back to Tetes des Morts. The dented sports car tailgated him, though weaving around. Fortunately, there wasn't any traffic. More cautious people would probably take the longer, highway route to Tetes des Morts, not the hilly gravel roads that wouldn't see a snowplow until the next day.

On the second to last hill, some force suddenly pushed Daniel's foot down on the gas and the school bus jumped ahead much too fast. He was able to steer and control the bus, but in the rearview mirror he saw something lift the dented sports car behind him off the road and into the huge oak tree that had survived numerous encounters with impatient drivers.

Daniel stopped the bus, yelled at the kids to stay in their seats, and ran out into the snow storm. The snow quickly formed icicles on his eyelashes as large as the studs the bus also had on its tires. When he got to the tree, he saw that Suzette Jolly and Paul Palmer had been thrown out of the car. Their bodies lay next to the tree, both of them with heads bent at unusual angles. He grabbed their wrists but felt no pulses. His nonmedical opinion was that they were both dead.

He thought he felt or heard shrieks as the translucent faces appeared again in the sky, this time dragging away the translucent faces of Suzette Jolly and Paul Palmer, both of whom sported grotesque grimaces. He sensed terror from the two of them and relief and gratitude from the other faces.

Daniel shook his head. His responsibility was to get these kids back to the school grounds safely, which he did, slowly and cautiously. As soon as he got to the school, he ran in and used the nearest phone to call the Iowa Highway Patrol and report the accident. The parents waiting to pick up their kids were grateful that their kids were all right.

"I should have taken the longer way home," Daniel said to everyone who came to talk to him. "I must have underestimated the storm."

Then the chairman of the school board walked over to him. "My son said there was an accident," he said.

"Yes," Daniel said. "Mr. Palmer and Mrs. Jolly followed the bus in Mr. Palmer's car. We were almost back when their car slid off the road and into a tree. I stopped the bus and went over to see if there was anything I could do, but they were both dead."

"Why didn't Mrs. Jolly ride the bus?" Mr. Greeve asked. "As a chaperone she should have been in the bus."

"She just told me she wanted to ride back with Mr. Palmer," Daniel said, shrugging his shoulders. "I couldn't force her to get on the bus."

"Well, I assume the Highway Patron will clear things up, and they'll want to talk to you," Mr. Greeve said.

"I'll do everything I can to help," Daniel said.

"I know," Mr. Greeve said. "Now where are we going to find another science teacher and English teacher?"

Principal Jolly resigned and left town. Patricia Hammond was named the new principal. Daniel noticed how his band students no longer seemed beaten down or scared when they came to practice.

After the night of the accident, Daniel didn't have any more nightmares.

SHE AIN'T HEAVY

Anthony Ferguson

"Colin Jonas peered through the damp foliage toward the ancient ruin of a mansion. He had heard the rumours that the old rock legend had let the place go to pot, but this was worse than he expected. The manor house seemed to ooze and sweat a slimy discharge. Perhaps leftovers of the occupant's legendary decades of booze and pills, night sweats and DTs – or maybe Jonas was thinking more about himself.

The weather didn't help either. A thin sheen of rain powdered Jonas's face. Drops hung from his lashes. It pattered off the leaves and ran down the dark murky walls of the two-storey relic before him. He pulled his coat tighter. Hugging it to his wiry frame in a futile attempt to stave off the effects of the fast-approaching English winter.

The house hadn't always been a ruin. He had seen it featured in a prominent hard rock magazine in its eighties' heyday. Like its occupant, it had once been a glowing example of British achievement. A fine piece of seventeenth century architecture, built to last, a bit like the metal god who dwelled within its walls. The fallen idol Jonas intended to pay a visit to tonight.

The large ornate stone driveway, only slightly overrun with weeds, was conspicuous in its absence of vehicles. Where once, Jonas remembered from those same old rock magazines, sat a plethora of limousines and the shiny black edifice of the Devil's Gate tour bus, there was not a motor in sight. Surely the old boy wasn't that hard up he had to sell them all? Still, the absence of limos didn't necessarily mean the place was empty.

He crept up to the imposing front door, wide enough to admit a hospital gurney, and chancing his luck he gave the handle a twist. It opened with a creak. Jonas shrugged and slipped inside, closing it behind him. he found himself in what looked like a boot room.

From there he snuck around the lower floor, checking the kitchen, scullery, various sitting rooms and a small library, to ensure there were no staff still in attendance. The absence of chatter suggested, there were none. No cooks, no cleaners, no gardeners. How far the mighty had fallen.

Jonas spent a few minutes enjoying what was clearly the occupant's trophy room. Several dust-coated framed gold disks adorned the walls. Pictures of the band in their pomp, with various hangers on. Devil's Gate, all gone now to that great rock heaven in the sky, or in the Gate's case, perhaps the one down below for heavy metal bands. All gone bar the subject of this little visit.

He flicked though the LP record collection and smiled at the memory of some of the band's disks, recalling how, when and where he had first encountered them. Many through his old man's stories. Jerry Jonas having introduced his son to the eighties rock legends.

Opening another door, he found a set of stone steps leading downward to darkness. Jonas quickly closed the door again. The basement could wait. He hated basements. He had watched too many horror movies, knowing full well that according to lore, cellars were invariably the gateway to Hell.

Finding a half full bottle of whisky on a cluttered dresser, Jonas took a sniff and had a swig. The burn was good going down his gullet. He took another belt, felt his skin glowing. He swaggered across to the bottom of the stairs, and yelled, "You up there, Mr Crowley?"

Getting no reply, he shrugged and took another swig of the burning malt. The guy might be a faded star, but he still stocked quality booze.

"Yo, Ace. You here?"

The only response was the sound of falling rain on the weathered shingles. Cackling to himself as the rich liquor took effect on his innards, Jonas started up the winding stairwell. The walls here were also encumbered with mementoes of the occupant's glory days. Posters from gigs played long ago, and more photos of the dead band and the sole survivor's subsequent solo career, which itself had flickered brightly until age wearied the man and he faded away.

Ace Crowley, a cliched but apt pseudonym for a wild-haired rock god. Certainly more appealing than his birth name, Reg Smith. *Nobody was shelling out big bucks to hear Reg Smith belt out black metal classics eulogising Satan, that's for sure.*

Accessing the upper landing, he made his way from room to room, several dusty bedrooms revealing a sad lack of use, or a lack of groupies and various hangers on, the accoutrements of fame. The layers of filth also belied the absence of hired help. Two of the three upper bathrooms were similarly decrepit. The other just looked in need of a good scrub. The grubby vanity held a couple of empty bottles of scotch.

Finally, the worn carpet led him to what could only be the master bedroom. Jonas reached into his coat and pulled out the rusty filleting knife he'd found in the kitchen drawer of his latest doss-hole. Enough to terrify the occupant on the off chance he was in there, sleeping off a bender. He pushed the door open and crossed the threshold.

"Mr Crowley, I presume?" Jonas announced to the empty room. The dishevelled bed suggested recent occupancy, and the bottles on the bedside table confirmed he was in the right place.

He glanced around, taking in the contents. More gold records. *Might have to nab a couple of those. He won't miss them.* A combination safe, tall and solid, peeked out at him from an array of spandex and other remnants of a rock career from the depths of a large walk-in robe. Slipping the knife away, and cracking his fingers, Jonas made his way across to it, like a spider to a fly, when something caught the corner of his eye and he swung around.

"Holy fuck!"

The figure stood across the room from him, hard against the wall. How had he not noticed it before? It seemed to blend into the garish wallpaper.

Jonas reached for his knife. He stared at the mute figure. It stared back.

The effigy had its arms raised toward him in a supplicating manner. Jonas squinted and looked closer. "Where the Hell did you come from?"

He wondered why it stood so mute and frozen. Jonas began to laugh.

"Well bugger me!"

He walked around the huge four poster bed to get a closer look.

He reached out and poked the woman, for it was definitely female, in its ample chest, marvelling at the give in the alabaster flesh.

Jonas reached up and pulled the dressing gown off the girl's shoulders. Beneath she wore only a flimsy negligee, which barely covered her generous curves and outsized breasts. The breasts were stuffed into an ill-fitting sheer black bra, almost spilling over the top.

She regarded him with large but lifeless mascara laden green eyes. Her full pouting bee-stung lips were slightly parted, revealing a set of gleaming white teeth. If she had lived, she gave the appearance of recent death. Yet live she did not, could not, never had. She was instead a perfect replication of somebody's ideal sexualised female form.

Jonas drew in a breath and shook his head. He reached out and squeezed her hand with its painted fingernails, marvelling at the verisimilitude of her touch. Just for a moment he imagined that she squeezed him back. He recoiled, and stepped back, but found the mild repulsion quickly subsumed beneath...what? Attraction, curiosity, desire?

"I know what you are," he said. "You're one of those new kind of sex dolls. Yeah, I've seen you on the Internet."

He sat back on the bed and admired her. In his regular solitary onanistic meanderings around the world of Internet pornography, Jonas had occasionally stumbled across advertisements for these new twenty-first century iterations of the old inflatable rubber dolls. However, he had never seen one in the flesh, so to speak, or the silicone, or whatever marvellous substance this work of art consisted of. He knew they were bloody expensive, only within the financial reach of the most well-heeled of perverts.

"Do you talk?" he asked her, to be met with her eternal silent stare. Her brilliant eyes seemed to observe him with a hint of disdain, her lips set in a fixed coquettish leer.

"No, I guess we haven't got that far yet, eh?" He smirked at her, glad to wrest back control of the monologue.

He stood and ran his fingers across her cheek and around the back of her silken hair.

"You can stand on your own two feet. That's impressive." He leered at her. "Still, I'm sure you're more useful when you're horizontal."

Jonas peered at her sheer black panties and reached out with a glint in his eye.

"Let's have a look at you then."

He pulled the nylon restraint forward and eased the panties down over her wide hips.

"Oh wow!"

The doll's sex organs had been skilfully and majestically crafted. The inner and outer labia perfect in the rendition of permanent arousal. The pudenda swollen and a darker shade of pink. Unable to resist, Jonas ran his fingers down her manufactured slit, flicking the doll a guilty look, expecting her to protest, feeling like a naughty teenager again.

To his surprise, she was damp.

"Oh!"

He probed and slid his middle finger inside her, seeking out and finding the perfectly rendered clitoris.

"Well. You're full of surprises." He withdrew. "I bet our rock God gets a great deal of satisfaction out of you."

He reached up and slid a sticky finger between her lips. Surprised to see the mouth widen to admit him. Even her tongue was exquisite in its craftsmanship. Whoever made these objects of desire certainly put their heart and soul into the work.

Jonas let out a squeal as he felt her lips close around his finger, and he jerked his hand back automatically, as if anticipating a bite.

"Jesus!"

She looked at him doe eyed, her mouth still forming a perfect circle. A look of recognition crossed his face.

"Oh, I get it. You're a goddamn android! High functioning sex toy." He slid his finger back between her red lips and cooed as he felt her gently sucking on it. He felt himself begin to stiffen and withdrew the digit.

He took in her whole form again, head to toe. Almost shocked to find himself short of breath. "Jesus! I can see why blokes..."

Jonas reached out and pulled the doll toward him, pushing his body against hers. His erection straining at his greasy pants and rubbing against her bare rounded midriff.

"What the fuck are you doing?"

Jonas almost leapt out of his skin.

He spun to find himself confront by a legend. Ace Crowley in the flesh, or at least what was left of it. The rock god stood in the doorway, clad in an unforgiving pair of tight black leather pants and a faded black t-shirt promoting his European tour of 1991. The years had not been kind. The leather of the bikers' jacket hanging off his narrow, drooping shoulders looked as old and battered as Crowley. Jonas couldn't help but notice that above the sunken cheeks and bloodshot pin-prick eyes that the once lustrous flowing black mane had retreated back well over the ridge of his crown and had turned an ashen grey.

"Mr Crowley," Jonas stammered. I'm a huge fan."

"Never mind that bollocks," the rock legend growled in his native East End drawl, "What are you doing in my bleedin' house, and what were you about to do wif my Lily?"

"Lily?" Jonas turned and gave the doll and accusing look. "This thing?"

"She's not a thing. She means the world to me. You keep your 'ands off her." The ageing rock god took a step toward Jonas, who raised his hands and backed away.

"Easy does it, old mate. It's not her I came for." He pulled out the knife. That stopped the angry rocker in his tracks.

Crowley backed away, raising his hands before him. "What do yer want wif me?'

Jonas grabbed an old wooden chair from one side of the bed and dragged it across. "That's more like it, Ace, or should I call you Reg? Why don't you sit yourself down here, and we'll have a little chat?"

The rocker reluctantly did as he was bid. Jonas took a closer look at the fallen idol. Hard to imagine this wasted relic once commanded audiences of tens of thousands of dedicated fans.

"What happened to your hair, Ace? Last time I saw you on stage, you had a beautiful head of hair."

Crowley scowled. "I got old, you moppet."

"It was only about eight years ago."

The rocker's eyes narrowed. "Eight years... the Fallen Angels tour? That was a bloody wig."

"Oh. I couldn't tell."

Crowley gave a half smile. "Tricks of the trade. Wigs, 'airpieces. I even had a weave at one point. Didn't take. Course the technology is much more refined these days. Look at Elton... Anyway, wot the bladdy hell are you doing on my manor?"

"I'll ask the questions, Mr Crowley." Jonas gesticulated with the knife. "You can guess why I'm here. You've got something I want. Cash, moolah, filthy lucre. I've heard all the rumours. How you never trusted the banks. Got all your money holed up here with you." He pointed the tip of the blade over Crowley's shoulder. "I'm guessing it's in that safe over there in the closet."

They both turned toward the closet. Crowley shook his head. "Nothing much in there these days."

Jonas gave a bitter smile. "Nevertheless, I would still like to take a look for myself. You see, Ace old chum, I've got myself into a bit of a pickle. I owe some nasty men rather a lot of money, and I figured you could see me right with a small donation."

The rocker snorted, "Here we go, another bleedin' sob story. Some things never change. Always somebody looking for a bladdy handout. Wot is it, gambling, drugs?"

"Bit of both," Jonas shrugged. "So, if you would just be good enough to give me the combination of that little beauty over there, I'll be on my way and out of your hair.... What's left of it."

The old rocker shook his head. "How much do you owe these thugs, son?"

"Does it matter? About fifty grand, and I'll take a bit more for my troubles."

Crowley chewed his lip. "There ain't fifty grand in there, pal."

Jonas sighed. "Look, old man. I know you're stalling. Just give me the combo and let's get this over with, and you can get back to shagging the arse of your little mannequin missus here, to your heart's content." Jonas glanced at the doll as he spoke. Was she staring at him?

A sudden memory slid its way to Jonas's frontal lobe. "What did you call her? Lily? Wasn't that the name of that infamous groupie that used to follow you around on every tour?"

"Yeah. Lily the lush. I bleedin' loved that gal."

"I heard you all did, and half the road crew as well."

Crowley's face hardened. "You watch your mouth, pal. You don't know the first thing about love."

That drew a laugh from Jonas. He waved the knife in front of the rocker's nose. "Oh, that's rich, coming from a bloke who shacks up with a bloody doll."

Crowley sneered. "Yeah, look at yer, big lanky streak of piss. You've never loved and been loved, I can tell. You don't know nuffin' about women. Lily might've been a slag, but she had a heart of gold. Loveliest little gal I ever met. I should've married her."

"Oh please, Ace," Jonas laughed, "spare me the sordid details of your infamous gang bangs. Enough of the banter, sunshine. Are you gonna give me the combo, or do I have to start cutting?"

This time Crowley snorted. "You 'aven't got the bollocks, son."

Jonas's hackles rose. He juggled the knife from one hand to the other and swung his fist into the old rocker's face. Crowley's nose snapped with an audible crack.

"Oh, yew fucker!" Crowley raised his hands to his bloody nose and spat through a mouthful of blood.

"I'm sorry, Ace. I don't want to hurt you."

"You coulda bloody fooled me!" The rock god wiped his streaming eyes.

Jonas spied a box of tissues on the dresser and passed it over. "Here. Don't make this any harder, Ace, just give me the combination."

"Fuck you!" Crowley dabbed at his crooked nose.

Jonas sighed. He grabbed the rocker's left hand and yanked it toward him. He pulled the old man's digits out straight and poised the rusty blade over his index finger.

Crowley shook his head from side to side. "No...no...don't do it, son."

"How would it feel to never pluck a guitar again, Ace?" Jonas raised his voice an octave.

"No!"

"Don't make me do it!"

"I can't give yer the combo..." Jonas saw the old man's wild eyes flicker toward the doll and back.

"So help me, I'll cut it off..." Jonas had a sudden thought and swung the knife around toward the doll. "I'll cut her. How would you like that? I'll gut her."

"Please, no...".

"Let's see what she got inside." Jonas yelled. He raised the knife and positioned it over one of the doll's erect nipples.

"Don't hurt her."

The words only further enraged Jonas. "Hurt her? She's not fucking real, you old goat. She's made of fucking silicone." He gave a bitter laugh. "She can't feel pain. Here, look." Jonas swung a roundhouse punch and knocked the doll off its feet. It crashed to the floor.

"NO!" Crowley screamed.

Jonas lifted his boot above the doll's face, ready to bring it down with force. He looked back at Crowley.

"1-9-5-9-6-6-6."

The foot hovered, then lowered.

"That's better."

Jonas pocketed his knife, and moved across to the safe, pushing rows of old mouldering stage clothes aside.

He looked back at the rock legend. "Don't you fucking move!" He gazed back from the safe to the rocker as he worked. "6 6 6. I should've bloody guessed. What's the first bit represent?"

"Year I was born."

Jonas smiled as the safe gave an audible sigh and clicked open. Somehow, he sensed it was the first time it had opened in a long while.

"Aha! Here we go. Let's take a little look.... Ooh!"

He pulled an object from a stand nestled inside. Brandished the gleaming black and white guitar before him. "Oh my God! Is this the legendary Gibson Les Paul? The one from *Kings of the Underworld?*"

Crowley nodded. "The very same."

Jonas marvelled at the beautiful object. "Jesus! This thing must be worth a fortune. Isn't this the one you supposedly had on your lap when you met the Devil at them crossroads? Obviously, that was just a story."

"Yeah. Stories sell records, son. But there's an element of truth in every legend."

"Yeah, well I didn't see you die at twenty-seven, though. More like a hundred and twenty-seven."

"Some of us make different deals, sunshine."

"That right?" Jonas tossed the guitar onto the bedspread. "Well, it's no good to me anyway. Cold hard readies are what I need to solve my problems."

Jonas turned and reached back into the recess. Ah, here we go." He retrieved a smallish black tin and prised it open. Pulled out the wads of notes and flicked them through his fingers. He turned on Crowley.

"What's this? There's not even two grand here?"

The rock God sniffed. "Well, I did tell yer."

Jonas shook his head. "No, there's got to be more somewhere." He turned back to the safe and reached inside to something sitting further back, the last item held within. He pulled it out into the light. "What the fuck is this, a book?" He turned it over. There were words scrawled on the pock marked leather cover, but they were in a language he didn't understand.

Crowley's mouth curved into a sly smile. "It's a grimoire."

"A grim what? It's bloody grim all right."

"A grimoire, you ignoramus, is a book of black magic. It contains the names of demons. Tells you how to raise them and how to command them to do your bidding."

Jonas flicked though the ancient text, sneering at the strange words and diabolical images dotting the pages. "Oh, come on! You don't actually believe all this mumbo jumbo, Crowley? You said yourself in interviews the Satanic imagery was all for show."

"Yeah, what I said and what I believe are two different things, old son. Don't believe everything an artist tells yer."

"You expect me to believe this shit? You conjured up the fucking Devil, and what, sold your soul for fame and fortune? Come on!"

"In this very house."

Jonas waved the book. "Bullshit!"

Crowley's voice rose, his eyes sparkled. "The Prince of Darkness rose up. It was incredible."

"Oh, fuck off!" Jonas hurled the book at Crowley. It bounced off his chest and hit the floor with a dull thud.

"It's true. It's all true. The devil weaved his magic in song through me. All those tunes, all those money-making hits, he wrote through my hand. Made me his muse."

Jonas's voice rose an octave, verging on the precipice of hysteria. "What about the band? They in on this bollocks? Didn't help them. They're all fucking dead."

"Everyone has to make sacrifices. I had to make... choices. Had to fight to keep what I had."

Jonas shook his head. "You're not making a lot of sense, Reggie boy."

"Think about it, son. I had fame, I had money, but what did I not 'ave?"

"What?"

"Love, son."

Jonas saw the old rocker glance toward the fallen doll. "Oh, come on. You don't mean...?"

"Lily fuckin' died. Drug overdose." Crowley lowered his head into his hands. "I was heart-broken, desperate, wanted her back. It was complicated. There were incantations. It needed blood."

"Fuck off with this horse shit. Where's the rest of the money, you old charlatan?"

"There is none. I spent most of it on hookers and blow... the rest I just wasted." Crowley laughed bitterly at his own joke.

"So help me, old man, I'll..." Jonas rushed the metal God and slid his hands around the fallen idol's withered throat.

"Blood..." the ancient rocker spluttered."

"I'll bloody kill you..." Jonas squeezed tighter. Letting all the pent-up rage of his shitty life filter though his fingers. A steady flow of crimson from the rocker's busted nose oozed over his hands. He yanked the old man to his feet in a death grip. Crowley's eyes blazed as he looked over Jonas's shoulder and pointed, gasping, fighting to speak.

"No... don't!"

Jonas's foot slid on the cover of the grimoire at his feet. He kicked out angrily, squeezed his hands tighter round the old man's throat, watching his eyes widen and bulge in their sockets. Then he heard a loud crack and felt a sudden sharp pain, like a razor blade digging into his skull.

Jonas looked into the old man's face in confusion, to see it spattered with his blood. His grip loosened, and Crowley let out a coughing wheeze and staggered over to the bed. Behind Jonas, the life-sized doll raised the guitar and smashed it into the back of his head again.

Jonas crumpled to the floor and rolled over on his back. Above him, he saw the doll, impossibly alive, glaring down at him. Blood smeared its silicone features. Its mouth curled into a snarl. Somewhere inside him he felt a row of lights flickering out into darkness.

He opened his mouth to speak, to protest, but the doll raised the shattered guitar again and slammed it into his face. Deep in his mind, the music stopped for Colin Jonas.

Ace Crowley put a restraining hand on the doll's arm as she raised the weapon again. "Lily, Lily, Lily... that's enough, me darlin'."

When she did his bidding and retreated, Crowley bent to examine the wreckage. He picked through bits of splintered bone and gore and cradled the broken pieces in his arms. He shook his head slowly and quietly wept. Lily, standing aside, reached across and placed her cold hand on his shoulder.

Crowley heaved and sobbed. He turned to look at her, and held the shattered, blood and brain-soaked remnants up toward her pale, placid face. "Lily," he whispered, gazing into her soulless eyes. "How could you? Not the Les Paul."

THE SQUARE OF STARS

Laurence Klaven

It was a drizzly Monday, and the small crowd was distracted. As usual, it was made up mostly of tourists, so enraptured by the huge movie trailers that surrounded the Square—using new technology that made ads an actual part of the atmosphere, like clouds or birds or the rain itself—that it was hard to direct their attention to something as simple as a human being, even one who used to be famous.

Brad was philosophical about it, didn't stress, as the old expression went; his cool, after all, had always been part of his appeal, one way he could be identified if his face wasn't enough. Sometimes in his darkest moments, he felt his face *was* unmemorable, blandly handsome, interchangeable with any other actor's, and the only things that set him apart were his sandy blonde hair and perpetually flat stomach—no matter his age, the stomach was like a statue or a cobblestone street, the molded muscles like those rocks ("cob" meant "rounded lump," he'd read that somewhere). Don't be silly, Brad thought, he'd been talented, too, his nominations were proof; no wins, but how many handsome men had one? They only ever awarded ugly guys, they were the "artists"—and now he was being bitter, it was getting to him, being ignored while begging in the Square of Stars, and admit it, that's what he'd been reduced to doing, why mince words?

When he was ranting like this internally, he remembered— to further rub it in—that he wasn't even the original Brad, none of these problems or achievements had been his. He didn't have the memories of success and defeat that had tickled and tormented his ancestors, he had just the exact same face and body they had had, the same exact hand now extended for money, the thick rain coating his impeccable skin like cream.

"Hey!" he heard someone say. "It's him!"

At last, a tourist had seen him, really seen him, and was approaching. It was a woman (of course), middle-aged, middle-Western, middle-weight, who had been his fan in her youth, who had had his poster or his hologram in her room at home. She was way too young to have admired the original Brad, so it must have been one of the next or next *next* generation of Brads who had been her heartthrob. She pulled along her even more unprepossessing husband, as if to say, here's who I had wanted, here's who I had hoped to have, before I settled for you, before we settled for each other, here is my ideal. When she reached him, she was proprietorial, not deferential; she manipulated Brad like a mannequin, arranged him like a piece of furniture, fondled him like a photo in a phone or tablet she might have clutched to herself as a girl. As most of these women did, while her husband took their picture, she pressed herself against Brad, her breasts disappearing into his back or side, to punish her husband or excite herself or just to let Brad know she was available. This one stayed against him for a long time, long enough for her husband to get wise and say, "That's enough, Ingrid," or whatever her name was. The rain grew heavier and streaked her mascara, giving her a lived-in look that was erotic for a second, which surprised Brad, who usually felt nothing but pity for himself and these people while posing.

"Goodbye, sweetheart," she said, placing a hundred-dollar bill in his hand, and trailing her fingers down the sinewy muscle in his arm, sheathed in a shirt now growing sheer in the poisonous rain. "It was good to see you again."

"Good to see you, too," Brad said, and meant it, for it *had* been good, he had gotten as much as she had from the encounter, gotten a mild and momentary reassurance that he was who he said he was—was and wasn't, it was hard to explain.

"What movie was he in again?" he heard the husband ask, as the couple vanished into the irradiated rain and ads that erased them.

"I can't remember," she said, then guessed, "*Fighting Club*?" which was close enough.

Brad took refuge from the worsening storm in the lobby of a closed bank, the cash machine area where a homeless family huddled in sleeping bags. He turned and saw someone who for a second, he assumed was the clan's adult daughter. Then he realized it was another star; it had been hard to tell because her trademark blonde hair was darkened and curled by the rain and plastered against her face. She was new to the Square.

"Horrible weather," he said, to say something.

"Yes," she replied, less eager to engage with him than he would have imagined; she kept staring out the bank's filthy window and only glanced at him once. Brad had to remind himself that not everyone was a lonely housewife; other people in the Square were celebrities, too, no matter how far they had fallen from the original. Besides, she was younger than he, fifteen years at least, so maybe she preferred talking to men her own age.

Then, surprising him, still not looking, she extended her hand.

"Taylor," she said.

"I know." He shook it. "Brad."

"Right." Her eyes flickered over to him with fleeting good humor, just shy, he thought, or always being hit on and wary. He kept the conversation casual.

"Just started?"

"Yes."

"It's slow today."

"I did okay."

"Did you?"

"Yes. Different fan base from yours. Less worried about getting their wigs and toupees wet."

She was teasing him now, even though it was true, his people were, in comparison to hers, old. He smiled and she smiled back, this time actually turning from the greasy glass to see him. The sun emerged for a second, though the rain didn't stop, and lit up her face. It was almost corny how pretty she looked, as if the whole thing had been staged to set her off. Why had Taylor fallen out of favor over generations? The public was too fickle, Brad thought.

Then the room grew dull again. At the same time, each heard a rustle from the family sleeping feet away, near the shells of ATMs. One of them started whistling a Taylor tune—what was the name of it? "Shake" something?

"We love you!" a hoarse voice cried from the heap of fleece.

The girl smiled to show appreciation. Yet her expression was as streaked with sadness as the window was with rain.

"Let them pay for it," she whispered to Brad, in a surprisingly weary voice, linking them enough that he asked her out to lunch, on him.

They entered the Automat on the Square, one in a new chain of diners without servers, with only stations for credit cards, cafeteria-style troughs of soup, and be-clubbed security guards patrolling. They were waved at by a table of other stars, and while Brad wished they could be alone, he thought it impolite to demur. He led Taylor to them, and their trays bumped against each other, as their egos often did.

"How is everybody?"

As Brad and Taylor sat, he realized that this group of beggars was not on his or her level. They were not actual clones of celebrities designed to maintain—to keep recreating—their stardom over centuries. They were the experimental mix of one star with another, done in a desperate attempt to reinvent brands once it was discovered that no celebrity stayed hot forever, that the appeal of even a Brad or Taylor would eventually wear away, that even if your DNA was identical to a star's, you could still—at least figuratively—die.

There was an element of tacky sequel to these "blends"; they reminded Brad of the movie series manufactured in the nineteen-forties to recharge fading franchises, making Abbott and Costello meet Frankenstein, Dracula, and the Wolf Man. Or were they more like the monstrosities in H. G. Wells' *The Island of Dr. Moreau*, the story of the mad scientist who bred animals with men? He had a hard time looking at the Woody who had been mixed with himself, a man with kinky, thinning hair and glasses and Brad's own washboard abs who expressed comic observations too slowed by a stoner sensibility to make sense; or Bruce mixed with Michael, a half-hulking, half-elfin atrocity whose voice was at once a growl and a squeal, a sickening sound that made his singing unendurable. And about the blends of Cher and Prince, Meryl and Jack, Leo and the Grumpy Cat, the less said the better.

"Look who's here," Brichael (or Muce, as he was secretly nick-named) at once burred and purred, a soup spoon awkwardly held in his broad yet tiny hands. "Thanks for deigning to join us."

"Right," Chince (or Prer) boomed and whispered. "Thanks for *stooping* by."

As they laughed, Brad smiled, unpleasantly, used to this kind of rib. Yet he could see that Taylor was fresh to this freak show and made uncomfortable by it. Did she see the future opposite her in some revolting shape or form? He had heard that there were already blends of Taylor and someone—who, Miley? Kanye? That must have been it—on the drawing board or teething or a toddler. He wouldn't tell her: What good would it do to know she'd already been marked down?

"Can we go?" she whispered. "Let's go. I'm not hungry."

"Me, either," Brad answered, discreetly slipping a roll into his pocket; it had been more than a day since he'd earned enough to eat. As they fled, they were followed by the yowls and mews of the voices at the table, the song of things that should never have been.

The day had cleared up, and some streets were flooded, others utterly dry, as if the neighborhood had been picked up and tipped like a tray of melted ice (actually, there wasn't enough asphalt in existence for the amount of moisture dumped on the city these days). Brad watched Taylor parade around the puddles, humming unselfconsciously in a way he could only call enchanting. He understood how his own appeal had ebbed—people wanted another kind of man, softer, shorter, something—but how had hers? She should have been a perennial. He ran to catch her, and she cried out, comically—trilled was the word he wanted; she even sang when she was screaming, he thought. He caught her around the waist, her summer dress spun as she did, and her limbs—lithe, that was how she looked; it was the first time he had ever thought of anyone that way.

Taylor let herself be held by Brad, then placed her hands on his chest to steady them both as they came to a stop. There was something perfect about their pairing, and each was aware of it; the age difference aside, he had just enough heft on his side, she had just enough insubstantiality; each was the answer to the other and wanted to blend with the other, in the natural way. If their intimacy was automatic, maybe it was because they (falsely) felt they knew each other, as millions had felt this (falsely) about their earlier incarnations. In any case, they started toward Brad's apartment, which was in walking distance and had to be; neither carried enough cash for a cab.

Brad knew it was rumored that he smelled—that all the Brads had smelled, hadn't used deodorant, hadn't washed their hair. But it wasn't true: he kept clean, and Taylor attested to it now, approving of his aroma, inhaling deeply as she kissed his underarms and chest and moved down to the great gift of his gut, licking each small stone in his stomach, making marveling sounds about them before she undid his belt.

She took him in her mouth, and along with her movements her moans were rhythmical: love-making like music came naturally to her. Brad didn't want to finish, didn't know at his age if he could manage it twice, so without warning he lifted her onto his lap and she cried out, excited to be carried, and held the muscles in his arms as he somewhat roughly pulled down the straps of her sun dress, exposing her impeccably shaped, slightly blonde-downy breasts and kissed and bit her tense nipples as she grinded on his erection, which had remained hard since she'd made it so with her mouth, going faster and faster until she came, without him even being in her, without her underwear even being off.

"And that's just the beginning," Taylor whispered, slumping against him slightly. "That's how it's going to be with us."

She was right—it was just the start of their love-making that afternoon and evening and early morning. Brad was amazed by his own stamina, as if he had absorbed Taylor's energy, which seemed to be endless; she made love the way Taylors over time had carried on in their concerts, willing to entertain an audience until the sun came up and set again, calling other celebrities onstage to do duets, except now Brad was the only star moaning and making noise with her, finding variations in each rendition:

He was reminded of how earlier Brads must have said the same lines again and again, diversifying their delivery until the director felt one reading was the best, the way he and Taylor now finally got the most pleasure from the reverse cowgirl position, Taylor sitting over and over on him while turned away, spanking her own small behind on the hard surface of his wide thighs, each looking in the same direction, both of their faces in the clear as if posing perfectly for paparazzi, who weren't there anymore, who no longer cared about them.

While his anonymity had always consumed him, as he fell in and out of a drowse, Brad felt something new with Taylor: the hint of indifference to the person he was created to be, the place he was expected to occupy; he had an astonishing idea that just being someone's beloved might be identity enough. Huddled with her in his small apartment—which he hadn't had time to clean and the slovenly condition of which he was relieved she didn't mention—Brad saw himself for the first time doing other things and living somewhere else.

"As just a person," he whispered to her, "with a normal job. Maybe even fat and bald. Before I'm too old to be anything else. You know?"

Maybe it was his comparatively advanced age that had inspired this notion (the way that ambitious older men are calmer with their second families and don't neglect and abuse them the way they had their first), because Taylor seemed uninterested in the idea of retiring.

"You would never get fat," she said, touching his rigid flanks, "or bald," his dense thatch of hair, appearing to miss the point completely, he thought.

If anything, their connection made her *more* eager to parse their shared predicament, to express her anxiety about being perhaps the failed final one in her line, as if she had never explored it until now, for who else would have understood?

"Why is she—am I—no longer of interest?" Taylor asked, wearing only Brad's T-shirt, running her fingers over his sweaty, almost hairless chest.

Brad was struck by the ambition that had been masked by her unassuming façade; then he wondered whom he was fooling: he was not just an easy-going slacker, either, despite his persona.

"Don't drive yourself crazy," he said, as if he had not done so himself—about himself—for years.

"Too white? Too blonde? Too dull?"

"It's not a good use of time."

He felt Taylor withdraw from him then, shutting down, as if she'd been dismissed. He could feel it in the small shift in her position; he was sensitive to slights; all performers were. It panicked him; Brad knew now that his need of Taylor was greater than any aging quest for ease; that could come, if it ever did, later on. For now, he only wished to keep her close, and he tried to do so in the form of a confession. "I feel I've let everybody down. All the other Brads. That I've failed."

"Me, too." And she came back against him.

Soon, seeking to further soothe her, he rolled them a joint—something else Brad had always been said to enjoy to excess, a rumor which in this case was true—but given the extreme level of her agitation, the drug didn't do much good. Brad felt Taylor's tears scatter on his chest, like pesticide sprayed on pavement. He decided to introduce an alternative treatment for her upset, one he hadn't tried in years and about which he had no idea how Taylor would feel.

"I have a friend who brews beer," he said, and Taylor nodded, indifferently, of course, her head shake raining more tears into the valley of his clavicle. "He makes peast, too," he said, with calculated casualness, using an old acting trick (why let it all go to waste?). He meant the genetically altered yeast strain that mimicked poppies, which made possible cheap and mass-produced poppies from an original, as Brad and Taylor had been produced, though they were not synthetics, they were the real things.

Being young yet not innocent, Taylor sniffled and didn't say no, and Brad—using the doggedness of the actor he had been born as but never been allowed to be—took this as a yes.

Brad bought the homemade heroin from his friend, Alan, at the low cost of whatever he'd saved in a shoebox in his closet, plus a hand job Alan demanded become a blowjob right before Alan ejaculated, betraying Brad after he believed they'd made a deal.

"Beggars can't be, etc.," Alan said, holding Brad's head as it bobbed, knowing how little Brad liked thinking of himself this way (Alan was a commodities trader whose great-grandmother had been a fan of the original Brad and so kept this one around as a friend for fun).

That night, Brad and Taylor started by inhaling it, and Brad showed Taylor how to fire up the foil and keep it moving, then how to suck the fumes into her mouth like soup. He had forgotten how much he enjoyed doing it but seeing the powerful pleasure it gave Taylor brought it to a whole new place, and the good feeling it gave him about how it tethered them together was greater than his guilt for initiating her.

Brad was too weak not to want more, which was the reason he'd stopped in the first place. Soon this pleasure wasn't enough for him or took too long, and they started sharing a spoon (swiped from the Automat), a lighter (taken from a tourist), a tie (one of Taylor's costumes, an homage to a movie—"Annie" who?—made by Woody before he was blended with Brad), and putting the drug into veins which became like the streets coursing with dirty liquid that they walked and begged upon.

Then it had been weeks since they'd made love, even though they had so enjoyed doing it, but this was better and, anyway, made it impossible for Brad, though Taylor, too, had started to lose the girlishness that had caused her sexual avidity to be so unexpected and erotic; she noticed and lamented the loss, Brad could tell, it wasn't just him. But that didn't make them stop, that was out of the question.

When Brad and Taylor worked the Square now, they did so with new desperation, because they needed so badly what the money would buy. This changed their behavior in ways that got them *less* of what they wanted: those who wished to be photographed with Taylor needed her to be fresh, pretty and, above all, nice, and she couldn't be any more, looking stringy and not slim, singing in a cracked and phlegmy falsetto, snapping at them to shut up and get on with it, and why was that a fifty, not a hundred, what, were they poor, they didn't look poor, your fanny pack alone must have cost fifty bucks at least, for fuck's sake, and Brad, far from being cool, was belligerent and threatening, slapping a camera from a husband's hand when he'd had enough shots or pushing away a woman pressing herself against him, self-conscious about how un-muscular he must feel now, his stomach for the first time vague and undefined, as if someone had taken a knife and scraped all his abs into the street, a few flying off on their own and shooting into a subway grate or something.

At least they did this together, that's what Brad told himself, as he and Taylor fell asleep at night or in the afternoon or the late morning, in each other's stained and skinny arms, now shadows, as the old expression went, of themselves.

"Wake up," Taylor said, a week (or a month) later. She was shaking him. "Wake *up.*"

Brad managed to open his eyes, confused as to where he was. He had been dreaming that he was the original Brad and attending the Oscars; on his arm was not Taylor but the original's wife, an actress who had not lasted long enough in the public imagination to be recreated; it was arbitrary who remained famous and who did not, he thought. Understanding his actual circumstances—sleeping slumped where he'd last sat, on the floor near the coffee table—was a painful comedown. Still, there was Taylor staring down at him, at least Brad had her, what was left of her, anyway, in his quest to keep her: Today she looked particularly peaked and smelled of sweat, beer, and something else. Rust? Was that it?

"I've got good news," Taylor said.

"What's that?"

"They want us."

"Who? For what?"

"For a film. We've got an offer for a job. To play ourselves."

For a second, Brad didn't reply, the sentences so foreign to most he had heard in his life. He straightened up and stood, and the action forced him to focus, the words coming closer and becoming clear, like oncoming cars, but in a good way, bringing him food when he'd been famished.

"Really?" It was the best he could do, his lips were so dry. Excitedly, he clutched her wrist and for the first time truly perceived how thin it was: his spidery fingers crawled up her starved forearm; he was appalled at what he'd done to her.

"Yes," she said. "I worked while you slept. I met an actual producer. They're small parts, but..."

Brad nodded. What act had she performed for them to get so lucky? Maybe nothing; maybe she had more pride than he. He would never ask, so he would never know.

"When? When?" was all Brad *did* ask.

"In six weeks," Taylor said, implying they had only that long to become themselves again, there was no time to waste.

Taylor decided to go cold turkey, which she believed she was young and strong enough to do. Brad opted for warm turkey, using Xanex and Oxycodone he again had to get from Alan, who this time demanded only that he beg, repelled as he was by Brad's physical condition. The regimen solved nothing, since Brad started taking *all* of the drugs, and Taylor—whose withdrawal had been quick and relatively painless—insisted that he attend a clinic where they administered Suboxone, This drug mimicked the effects of heroin the way the peast mimicked the poppies and Brad and Taylor did *not* mimic the originals, because they *were* the originals—oh, forget it, Brad thought, he was not thinking clearly about anything now.

And, of course, Brad found himself addicted to the Suboxone, too. It made him nauseated, his pee dark and his eyes yellow, which meant that it had given him liver damage, which sent him to the hospital where, despite everyone's best efforts, in the space of several weeks, he died, saying, as Taylor wept beside him, "I wanted so much to live, with you." As a final indignity, the chart at the foot of his bed misspelled his last name as "Zitt," as if he had been but a blemish upon and not—as his actual last name suggested—the core of the original star.

When Taylor returned alone to the Square, she found herself the object of sympathy from the other celebrities. Most of them were motivated by *schadenfreude*, she felt, and secretly relieved that Brad's and her relationship had been squelched; she had never been as sentimental or idealistic about life as she looked. (Taylor had heard nothing from the film producer since Brad's death; he had not even shown up to say he was sorry.)

Only Brichael (or Muce) seemed genuinely put out by Brad's passing; to her surprise, the blend even offered her a couch in his apartment when she was evicted. Though Taylor had stayed clean, fewer and fewer fans wanted photos; while she could gain weight and wash and color her lifeless hair, her lack of spirit appeared permanent. It wasn't just the drugs; Taylor felt that the loss of Brad's love, the first real love in her life, had aged her like an illness. And forget singing: she had a laryngitis caused by her having been crushed: her fading life force was taking her talent with it.

Still, one day, when she saw the young producer walk swiftly as if escaping across the Square, she made sure to make the effort to accost him. (Taylor had done nothing with him except wear no underwear and lift her skirt as he touched himself, so she had nothing to regret.)

"He said he'd been thinking about me," she told Brichael later, in his apartment. "But I'm sure he was lying."

"So what?" Brichael shrugged, with his usual gruff gentleness. "Life's full of indignities. Get used to it, girl."

Taylor told him the rest: how the producer said the movie scene had been altered to erase Brad but—if she were still interested—she *could* be seen for a second on a TV in the background, as the original Taylor in an old clip (it was cheaper to film a fake clip than lease a real one). The problem, the producer said directly, was that, because of her self-abuse, Taylor now looked older than the original had at her peak, and the makeup budget was too small to make a difference. If she could come up with an answer, the part—and the one day of non-union work—would be hers.

Taylor sat on the bed while Brichael loomed above her. She leaned her head hopelessly against his thick left leg, which was sturdier and more comforting than his spindly right one. "It's too late," she said, with unprecedented despair. He reached down and with his full and skinny fingers stroked her face.

"It's not," he said. "I know something that'll make you as good as new."

After Brichael explained, Taylor was too grateful for words and ashamed of having initially judged him on appearances alone. Yet she had no money to pay for dinner, let alone something as expensive as this.

"It's okay," he said. "You'll just owe me a little more." And his high-low laugh told her he intended to hold her liable for nothing.

Not long after, at a private clinic, Taylor had performed on her a simple plastic surgery she was assured would restore the youth and freshness that had been lost from her face, a way to recapture at least some of the essence of the original.

When the bandages were removed, Brichael waited with excited impatience. Yet before she looked at her face, Taylor could tell from his that something wasn't right. Still, he tried to shrug it off.

"It'll be fine," Brichael said. "Everyone looks like hell at first."

But while the inevitable swelling went down, Taylor's cheeks had been left permanently uneven, and her lower eyelids were stubbornly lumpy.

"The doctor said the fat grafts from your lower back would *work*," Brichael said, with dismay. "You know, for your tear troughs."

Her strange new look made Taylor ineligible for the movie job. She returned once more to the Square, where she was met with confusion and derision from tourists and celebrities and dismissed as an imposter. To all of them, she looked like a star who had never been born rather than one born and born again, a fact which disoriented her.

Today, Taylor continues to wander the general area, speaking to the absent Brad, singing to a non-existent crowd. But she no longer feels allowed to enter the Square of Stars—the name of which denotes the number of a star multiplied by itself, something she had never understood until now, and the realization of which might have been the last rational thought of her steadily unraveling mind.

THE GIRL WITH CHARTREUSE HAIR

Terry Sanville

The crowd cheered wildly when Stan Belts drove his #12 Late Model across the finish line at the Santa Maria Speedway, nosing out his cross-state rival from Stockton. Before the winged sprint cars could be pushed onto the dirt track for the next event, Carl left his seat and headed for the beer booth.

He'd been sitting by himself in the grandstand's top row for two hours, breathing in high-octane gasoline fumes. A horde mobbed the beer booth, eager to refill their 16-ounce cups. Carl removed his earplugs and shook his head. The world seemed too loud, and he felt woozy from the fumes.

In the sea of grease-stained baseball caps, bald heads, and a few ponytails a swatch of bright color caught his eye. A girl with ragged hair the color of almost-ripe lemons stood at the counter and ordered. She turned toward Carl, a cup of beer clasped in each hand. Their eyes met and she smiled. Carl frowned. Holding two cups of beer meant she'd obviously come to the races with some gearhead boyfriend. But then he felt stupid for thinking otherwise.

She pushed toward him. The crowd seemed to magically give way. She stopped in front of Carl, leaned forward and kissed him on the lips.

"Come on, darlin'. We gotta hurry before the next race starts."

"Ah . . . do I know you?"

"Don't just stand there, come on."

She walked ahead of him, her curvaceous butt clad in skin-tight jeans, her sequined tank top showing plenty. Strange colored tattoos covered most of her upper arms and shoulders with mathematical notations and word fragments. Her chartreuse hair moved like a beacon through the crowd. Carl followed her back to his seat.

"How did you know . . .?"

"I've been watching you," she said. "You look different than the rest."

"Thanks for being kind and saying 'different.'"

"Where I come from, you'd be the handsomest one there."

Carl grinned and bowed his head, his face burning. "Not many women would kiss a man they don't know."

"Yeah, so?"

"Don't get me wrong. I'm not complaining."

She turned sideways on the bench and faced Carl. "Who wears a blazer, slacks and tie to a dirt track race, anyway?"

"I used to come here as a kid. I've got some . . . some time now. I teach advanced physics at the University."

"Yeah, I figured. Go ahead and drink your beer before it gets warm."

"Thanks. Here, let me pay you for the suds."

"Forget it. We'll settle up later. So, aren't you gonna say something?"

"About what?"

"My hair. Do ya like it or hate it?"

"I'm sure I'll love it the more I get to know you."

"Good answer. It's natural, you know. No dyes."

Carl scoffed. "Come on. You must have an interesting gene set."

"My name's Alcina."

"I'm Carl."

"Cool."

"Did . . . did you come here by yourself?"

Alcina grinned. "Nah, my friends are hanging out in the pits. One of them has a car that ran in Showroom Stock."

"Did he win?"

"No, she didn't." Alcina smiled, slid her arm around Carl's waist, and leaned her head on his shoulder.

She smelled like lemon blossoms on a hot August morning. He turned his head and kissed her, her dark eyes closed, pale lips parted. He half expected to wake up in his room at the Travel Lodge Motel where he'd been holed up for the past week, ever since his wife kicked him out. *This is some kind of waking dream* he thought. But when he opened his eyes after the kiss, Alcina smiled at him. Her hair burned in the late afternoon light.

In a tight three-column formation, the field of Outlaw Sprint Cars circled the track, waiting for the green flag to drop. The roar from their 900-horsepower engines made conversation impossible. Carl replaced his earplugs. Alcina pulled her ragged hair over her delicate pierced ears. The grandstands shook as the crowd stood to watch the start. Twenty-one methanol-powered racers shot forward, their roar loud enough to distract motorists on the nearby freeway.

Carl and Alcina held hands and watched. With only a third-of-a-mile oval track to work with, the sprint cars did more sliding into corners and slamming into each other than flat out racing. Methanol fumes burned Carl's eyes and he dabbed them with a tissue. Alcina sat upright and stared wide-eyed at the racers, mascara-laden tears streaking her pale cheeks; she looked like a beautiful female version of Alice Cooper. Carl offered her a tissue, but she ignored him.

After several spectacular crashes and race delays, about half the field crossed the finish line, exited the track and shut off their engines, their silence deafening.

With tissue in hand, Carl turned to Alcina and said, "Here, let me."

He wiped the black tear streaks from her cheeks, wetting the Kleenex to remove smears. Her lips trembled and she kissed him hard, her entire body shuddering.

"You . . . you really like racing, don't you?" Carl murmured.

"Yeah, the power of machines . . . "

"Huh. I felt the same way once. But my interest shifted to larger forces: energy, matter, gravity, cosmic inflation, that kinda stuff."

"Yeah, those things are really cool. But the rumble of race cars does more for me, turns me on."

"Ah, and I thought it was my professorial personality."

She laughed and kissed him on the nose. "Come on, let's get outta here."

"What about your friends?"

"I told them not to expect me back."

Carl smiled. "Pretty sure of yourself, aren't you?"

"Is that a problem?"

"No, no."

In silence, they drove in Carl's Prius to the never-closed Denny's in Pismo Beach. Carl ordered coffee; Alcina ordered a Grand Slam breakfast with extra bacon.

"So, do you live around here?" Carl asked.

"No. I'm from a planet far away."

Carl chuckled. "Ah, do all your citizens have chartreuse hair?"

"Yeah, mostly. But the lucky ones have blue or purple hair; comes from cross-breeding with the Calcidites."

"Huh, all we have here on earth are a few redheads. Your home must be exciting."

"I suppose. So, what about you, how come you're out here trolling for babes since you're married?"

Carl remembered his wedding ring and grinned sheepishly. "Well, I'm living in a motel while my wife figures out if she still loves me. I suspect she doesn't."

"How'd that happen?"

"You really want to know?" Carl leaned back in the booth and fingered his coffee cup.

"I'm always interested in what attracts and repulses humans."

Carl laughed. "Yeah, *repulsive*, the very word my wife used."

"If you don't want to tell me, that's cool."

"She complains I'm married to my work . . . she's right . . . but then that's probably just an excuse."

"Yeah, it's easy to lie, especially about love or its opposite."

"So, what's your story?" Carl asked, smiling. "Have you been on earth long?"

"Not so long, maybe three of your years."

"Huh. Except for the hair you fit in well."

"Thanks, that's the idea."

"Do you have . . . a boyfriend?"

"Not here . . . and I've been gone too long."

Alcina warmed her hands around her mug of tea and gazed out the window at the black sky full of stars and galaxy clusters. Their silence deepened.

"So, what about your tattoos?" Carl asked. "I think some of the notations are part of calculating the red- or blueshift of stars or maybe vacuum decay."

Alcina smiled. "You're the first person to recognize them. I love cosmology."

Carl laughed. "Most humans think that's the art of making people beautiful."

"Cosmology and cosmetology are both beautiful."

"Well, you definitely don't need the latter. You're . . ."

Carl sat back and stared at Alcina's face. He could have sworn that her eyebrows were dark arches stretched across a perfect pale forehead. But now they matched her hair, blazing green-yellow. And her eyes had changed from dark to a hazel color. *Probably just fancy contact lenses,* Carl thought. *But the eyebrows; maybe I'm remembering wrong . . . sucked in way too much methanol fumes.* The blazing eyebrows made her look happy, accessible, more vulnerable.

They exchanged synoptic versions of their life histories, with Carl doing most of the talking and Alcina volunteering little. But when they talked science, Carl realized that she knew her stuff. She probed the depths of his knowledge and seemed to be mentally cataloging everything he told her. After a couple hours of intellectual sparring, they ended up debating which model of the universe's demise was most probable.

"Well, whichever one happens, our sun will die long before the universe does." Carl sat back, feeling smug about his pronouncement.

"Yeah, maybe *your* star will be gone. But mine . . ."

"Right, right, the one that warms your planet, far far away."

"Carl, you have some very . . . very useful ideas."

Carl grinned. "Thank you. That's high praise coming from a brilliant extraterrestrial."

Alcina didn't smile. She reached across the table and laid a hand on his arm. "We should go."

"Yes, we should." Carl noticed for the first time that very fine chartreuse hair covered the tops of her lower arms, giving then a golden glow when light flashed across them. Her eyes had turned the color of new pennies.

"Your . . . your hair is changing . . . and so are your eyes," Carl stuttered.

"Do you like them better now?"

"Yes. You're beautiful."

"Good. Let's go."

"Ah . . . to my place?"

"Sure."

Carl hurriedly dumped some cash onto the table, and they left the almost empty restaurant. He felt awkward, not having been with a woman other than his wife for more than a decade. They drove in silence to the motel. Inside, Carl apologized for the mess and hurriedly straightened the bed covers. The lights clicked off. Alcina had removed her clothes. Her hair glowed in the dark, a bit disconcerting, but it made navigation easier.

They made frantic love until every bone in Carl's middle-aged body ached from his effort to keep up. Spent and out of breath he collapsed onto his pillow. With Alcina's head resting on his chest, he fell fast asleep.

A strip of morning sun shone through the curtains and cut a light path across the motel room. Carl woke to an empty bed. He checked the bathroom. Alcina had fled, leaving nothing behind but memories of the day before. He dressed and walked to the motel's lobby where a free continental breakfast awaited. The manager brewed a fresh pot of coffee and bad him good morning.

"Say, you didn't happen to see a young woman this morning with chartreuse hair?" Carl asked *sotto voce*.

The manager grinned. "No, sure haven't. And I would remember something like that."

Carl nodded and fixed himself a bowl of bran flakes and coffee. During the following week he couldn't stop thinking about Alcina. His graduate class in astrophysics seemed dull and incomplete without her agile mind probing his knowledge, pushing him toward a better understanding of the cosmos.

Carl drove to the Speedway on Friday night and sneaked into the pits, asked the gearheads if they'd seen her. Most just laughed when he described Alcina as the girl with yellow-green hair. He retired to the Denny's restaurant, sat in a booth and tried to remember what quadrant of the night sky had dominated her attention. His own image reflected in the window glass. He stared, wide-eyed. The ends of his hair had turned chartreuse. By the next day he'd become one of them.

THE GYRE

Samuel Finn

Manda steps carefully along the metal grating of the gangway ramp, always wet, always slippery. The littered ocean foams beneath. On both sides of her conveyor belts clatter up from the scoop of the bow and into the ship. Across the middle belt is another ramp and beyond that the third belt, all three carrying debris from the water into the vast maw of the ship as it churns through the endless swirl of trash surrounding them.

"Ears on, Lucas," she yells at the belt tender nearest her, ghost-like in the morning mist, a hooded druid in his yellow raingear. He is her brother, who now ignores her, or so it seems. Maybe he can't hear her in the din of the clanking belts, but she suspects he can. He is a troubled soul, often haughty, angry, especially with her, something she has never understood. His

sister, perhaps she knows him too well. The ship has its misfits—
the work attracts them—and he fits right in.

"Lucas!" She cuffs his shoulder. He turns with a sidelong
glance, wet stringy hair hiding his face. "Ears on," she shouts
over the clatter. She taps her own ear muffs, holding his gaze,
deadpan. It's for your own protection, she doesn't say, and rules
are rules. He knows these things. She gestures to the other
three tenders, all wearing the bulbous orange headsets.

One of them, Sarah, working across the belt, meets
Manda's gaze. She nods, with the hint of a smile, then nods
again at Lucas, tapping her headset.

Slowly he hoists his into place, grudgingly, then turns back
to the belt, saying nothing.

Two belt tenders work from each ramp, sorting through the
dripping junk brought up from the restless sea. With short poles
they watch for sea life, living or dead: fish, octopi, dead sea-birds
are common, often tangled in netting that needs cutting away.
They slide the creatures, living and dead, off the belts to drop
back into the sea.

Occasionally the injured ones, dolphins or other large
species who might survive, are brought back to the small fish
rehab pool on the stern deck. Manda's friend Shira serves as
fish doctor, but there's little she can do. They often they die
anyway, the pool water sloshing back and forth with the motion
of the ship. It's a sad business.

Manda doesn't like this part of the job, belt boss. She was
happier simply working the belts. This is what she gets for being
good at it. She squeezes past Lucas, down the gangway towards
the bow. The ocean swell gives the ship a heavy rocking motion.
A cold breeze blows mist at her face, and of course the smell,
rotting garbage, rotting fish tangled in the endless nets.

The broad scoop that forms the bow slices into the
ceaseless layer of trash, a few feet below the surface. The three
belts rise from the water bearing whatever floats onto them,
draining the cold north Pacific back through their latticework.

Two net wranglers stand on the cross ramp above the belts with their long poles. Abandoned fishing nets make up half the debris of this vast floating island, holding it together as the ocean current swirls around them, the gyre.

It's hard work. As Manda watches, Mateo hoists the free end of a heavy cable net up to an overhead grapnel, hangs it on the forbidding hook, then with a gloved hand punches the signal box that hangs from his belt.

With an answering beep, the chug of the winch motor sounds overhead, pulling the dripping net free of the belt and onto a wide rolling drum out of sight on the deck above.

Mateo moves under the thick green cords of the net as it rises, bowing his head to let his yellow souwester hat take the dripping seawater. With their poles he and Silas, the other wrangler, clear tangled trash and debris onto the belts below.. The dark shape of a fish rises out of the water, likely dead. Mateo hits his signal box again and the net stops rising.

Manda watches for movement of the fish as he works to free it. But it drops limp onto the belt below, maybe a grouper, the color gone from its scales. Mateo glances at her, nods toward the water below. She nods back with a thumbs up. He stabs the creature with his pole and slides it off the belt, a heavy thing. It splashes down.

Silas waves at her. "Manda," he calls on his headset. "We gotta stop forward motion. This is a big net."

She waves assent. Such a net, a heavy purse seine, likely from a factory trawler, might be a mile long, a huge thing that will drag beneath the moving ship, possibly tangle with the bow scoop, the stabilizer jets, even the twin screws that drive the ship.

"Bridge," she calls. "We got a big net down here. Request full stop."

She listens carefully on her headset. In the clatter of the belts, the grind of the net winch and the ocean breeze it's easy to miss headset dialogue. She is uncertain which officer is at the con.

"Yes, Miss Manda," she hears. It is Kotaama, the first mate. "We will stop."

The forward motion slows, then stops altogether as Kotaama backs the ship. Overhead the whine of the winch increases as it takes the weight of the net. Two tenders move along their gangways toward the bow to help clear the net.

How can a trawler simply leave such a net behind, Manda wonders. It must cost thousands.

Lucas makes no move to help. He turns and stands gazing out to sea, a gray sky over dark restless water. He has developed a fascination for the serenity of it all, the ocean, the sky, the stars at night, the occasional living creatures they are able to salvage from the nets.

It is a troubled serenity to Manda, troubled by the surrounding miles of trash, this gyre—a word she has learned—this expanse of swirling refuse, the endless flow of plastic trash slowly dissolving into microscopic bits that have become part of all living creatures, the fish, all the sea creatures, the land animals, all humans.

But the overarching beauty of it appeals to her brother, here at sea, has calmed him from the frantic, erratic creature he was back in Seattle. Her mission in bringing him to the ship has partially born fruit, at least kept him from trouble, from jail, from the street drugs and the psych wards and the medicines that seemed little more than trial and error, from doctors poorly hiding their disgust with Lucas and simply throwing prescriptions at him.

She watches as they work to clear the debris tangled in the rising net, yards of seaweed, scarred buoys, a broken chair, some metallic thing, bent and twisted, and the fish. They are mostly dead. She sees a small dolphin corpse, several yellowtail, a couple still alive. An octopus drops from the cables onto a gangway, then slithers off into the water below.

Manda moves back into the ship. Inside, two more tenders wait between the belts where they dump their debris into a cargo container below. With long poles they distribute the junk evenly in the huge steel box, but now they stand idle, the ship stopped. Only the debris from the net reaches them.

"You guys okay?" Manda asks.

"What's for lunch, boss lady?" Irene asks with a grin. It's a standing joke.

"I hear the galley has a new flavor of spam," Manda answers, "microplastic mixed with seaweed."

"Thought we had that last week."

"That was seaweed mixed with microplastic," Ned says, the other tender. His bright red hair tangles about his headset. "How big's that net?" He nods toward the bow.

"It's big," Manda says. "Gonna be a while. One of you can take a break if you want."

She moves on to the galley where a few of the nightshift still linger. "How was your night?" she says, pausing by their table.

"Dark," Ignatius replies, leaning his head on one hand. "Wet, smelly."

"You mean like every night?"

"Pretty much. Why're we stopped?"

"A big net," Manda says.

"Seems like we're getting more fish in the nets," Irene says.

She's young, still the idealist, the believer. It's more than a job for her, Manda knows. She's in journalism school somewhere and here on the ship for the story.

"Dead fish," she adds.

Manda sighs. "Dead fish are better than no fish. At least they're still out there." She steps to the coffee bar and holds a mug to one of the big urns.

"Miss Manda." It is Matco's accented voice on her headset. "Can you come back to the bow? I want to show you a thing."

"Be right there." A thing, what does that mean? She leaves the mug behind and retraces her steps forward.

On a gangway ramp between the belts three tenders stand in a group, Mateo on the cross ramp just above them.

Lucas waves urgently to her, pointing. "Manda, check it out, this thing. What the hell is this thing?" He has that wide-eyed look, that urgent body language she hasn't seen in weeks, maybe months, since they boarded the ship.

On the stopped belt lies a mottled gray creature, two feet long, with a vaguely triangular head, a row of black pits where eyes might have been. Its muscular body looks lumpish, deflated, clearly dead and partially decayed. Rows of string-like tentacles tangle around it, many rotted and broken. She finds it evil-looking, a small monster. An odd smell rises from it, an irritating chemical odor, disturbing, like nothing she's smelled before.

"What is it?" Lucas repeats. "It's wicked. That's no damn fish. What the hell is it?"

Manda shakes her head. "I don't know what it is. It looks dead, that's for sure."

"Smells terrible," Sarah says, stepping back. "And it's hot." She holds out a hand, as if toward a hot stove. "Let's get rid of it."

"Yeah, just slide it back in the water," Manda says.

"But what is it!" Lucas is shouting now. "That's no damn fish. There's no fish like that."

She reaches to touch his shoulder, but he shrugs her off with a convulsive movement, a movement familiar to her.

"It could be anything, Lucas," she says, purposely calming her voice, hiding her irritation at him, her embarrassment at her brother's near panic. "There's a lot of creatures deep down that we never see. It probably got dredged up somehow."

She glances up to Mateo. He's seen much, has been on the ship longer than any of them. He shrugs, shakes his head, gestures to move the thing back to the water.

"Give me your pole," she says to Lucas.

But he holds it away from her. "No, we can't just ditch it! Look at it!"

"Sarah," Manda says, motioning to her pole.

"Happily," she says. She spears the thing and slides it off the belt.

"Wait, stop," Lucas yells, grabbing for her pole, but too late.

The creature splashes down, its tentacles wave passively in the wash of water. A haze rises around it, a cloud of steam, then it slides beneath the surface.

"What's the matter with you, man?" Sarah yells at Lucas. "It's just some creature, maybe part of a creature, the insides of something. Why you getting all weird, Lucas!"

"Okay, okay," Manda says, gesturing. "Forget about it. It's gone. There's a lot of creepy shit down there. We got work to do. Lucas." She turns to him. "You need a break?"

His face resumes its usual sullen stare, and he shakes his head. "That thing was wicked," he mutters. "That wasn't just some fish. That smell...this whole place is wicked," he says, gesturing to the strewn ocean around them. "This whole fuckin' place. This shouldn't be."

"Yeah, well, that's for sure," Manda says, watching him. "That's why we're here, trying to clean it up."

Lucas shakes his head and turns away.

On the bridge Manda finds First Mate Kotaama and Captain Bascomb. The ship's motion is worse here, higher up and with no way on. A row of lights wink on and off as the stabilizer jets in the hull struggle to minimize the pitch and roll.

Bascomb stands by the down-angled bridge windows, watching the net rising onto the roller hidden beneath them on the deck below. Two decks down are the bow belts and gangways.

"What was that all about?" he says, turning his bearded, weather-beaten face to Manda. He's short, heavyset, with an air of tired authority.

She shakes her head. "Nothin' much, Sir. Just some weird creature, a very dead weird creature."

"Who's that tender? He's your brother, right?"

"Lucas," she says, "Yes, he's my brother. He can be a little emotional at times."

"Emotional?"

"Yes, sir. You may recall he's had some minor problems in the past. But he's worked out well on the crew." She doesn't want to say too much, hopes he remembers their initial interview, his consent to take him onto the crew.

Bascomb glances at Kotaama. "I have not seen such a creature," Kotaama says, "but hard to tell from up here." He is a big man, broad, athletic, his face and complexion reflect his heritage. Makah Tribe, Manda recalls, a sea-going people from Puget Sound. He wears his khaki officer's work uniform.

Manda shrugs. "I'm not even sure it was a whole creature. It looked pretty decayed and smelled really bad. Might have just been a random piece of something that died or got torn apart." She looks away, steps to the windows. "Are those belts back on?"

She doesn't want that thing identified, doesn't want to talk about it, or think about it. The smell from that thing, the evil look of it.

"Captain Bascomb," the intercom sounds. "Nav room here."

Bascomb clicks the button on the com box overhead. "What's up, Jake?"

"We got a radiation spike a few minutes ago. I didn't even notice till it printed out."

"A rad spike? Tell me more."

"It spiked up to three point six Grays for about five minutes, then dropped off. Back to baseline now. Whatever it was is gone."

"Thanks, Jake. Keep an eye on the sensor readouts and let me know if you get anything else."

"That's a lotta Grays, Sir. Dangerous for anyone nearby."

"Got it. Thanks, Jake." Bascomb turns to Manda, woolly eyebrows raised, then back to the com box. "Jake, one more thing."

"Yes, sir."

"Log your findings, but the crew doesn't need to know about this. Your eyes only."

A pause, then "Yes, sir."

'Anyone back there with you?"

"No, sir, just me." His voice is solemn with importance.

"Good man," the captain says.

He turns back to them, irritation on his face. "A rad spike, right when that thing was on the belt. You sure it was organic?"

"Well, Sir," Manda says, "it sure looked organic, like I said. We know there's radioactive waste out there. Maybe whatever it was got exposed somehow."

"You mean contaminated," Bascomb answers. "Those tenders were exposed, but only briefly." He sighs. "Okay, you heard what I said. This doesn't go beyond us. No need to rattle the crew." He eyes them in turn, serious, deadpan.

"Yes, sir," she and Kotaama respond.

"Now let's get that net on the roller and get moving again. The galley cooks don't like this kind of motion, and God knows we want to keep them happy."

Manda makes her way down to the fish pool. Contaminated, radioactive, she muses, a dead, decaying creature. She shivers at the thought of it's terrible smell. They were all exposed, but not for very long. She vaguely recalls one of the officers was designated radiation manager, but she can't recall who. The issue has never come up. She should find out who and talk to them. Ask Bascomb first, get his permission. She's the belt boss, those people are her responsibility. He won't like it, the hassle factor. He likes things to run smoothly. Maybe he needs another kind of ship, a small freighter or something.

The rehab pool is sunk into the stern deck. The hum of ventilation fans is loud here, the wide mouths of the vents just astern of the pool.

Shira stands hip deep in the sloshing water, walking a manta ray beneath the surface. A small dolphin idles around the edge.

"What's up, lady?" Shira says, with her perennially cheerful smile. "Why are we stopped?"

"They caught a big cable net. They're rolling it up."

"These guys hate this kind of motion. And the noise, especially that one." She nods at the dolphin. "If you stuck a sonar mike in here you could hear him squealing for his pod."

"He looks pretty healthy," Manda says. "Can't you let him go?"

"He's a baby. I'd hate to let him go now, with all that trash out there. And there's always sharks."

"How long can you keep him here?"

"I don't know. I wish we had a bigger pool. This is like a wading pool for these guys, wrong temperature, wrong food, no exercise. I'll have to let them go soon."

"There was some crazy looking thing that came up a few minutes ago. Really strange looking. Wish you could have seen it. And it was—" She stops, remembering the Captain's order. "It was creepy, weird smell. You know how smells can make you feel sometimes?"

"You mean like memories?" Shira says. "They remind you of childhood stuff?"

"Well, kind of, but the smell from this thing creeped me out. Not really a memory. Upset my brother, too."

"Lucas? I forget he's your brother. He's good with the fish. He comes back here and helps out sometimes. He's got a good heart."

Manda nods. "A troubled heart, but yes, he's—" Her headset beeps.

"Miss Manda." Mateo again. "We catch another one. Can you come?"

"Be right there." She turns back to Shira. "You want to come look at this thing? Mateo says they caught another one."

"Go ahead. I gotta feed these guys and then I'll come forward. Take some pics of it if you're going to toss it back."

On deck the day is warming, an angry sun is well up. The tenders have shed their raingear and again stand in a group below Mateo. The belts are stopped. The net hangs, dripping but unmoving. The roller engine idles above.

As she walks the slippery gangway she hears Lucas's loud jabber. He flails his arms. Beyond him another creature hangs in the net.

"Lucas," she calls to him as she approaches. "Lucas, would you calm down please."

He turns, hair plastered to his flaming face. "There's another one," he yells, pointing a shaky arm. "And it's alive. Look at that thing!"

She glances up at Mateo, who gives another gesture of pitching the thing overboard.

"And it's hot," Lucas goes on, holding his hands out. "I can feel it, and it's steaming."

It clutches a net cable, a bundle of its tentacles wrapped tight. As her eyes adjust to the glare, she sees the pits in its odd-shaped head are now glowing deep red. Are they pulsating? Steam rises from it and that smell comes to her again, that unsettling smell. And it might be radioactive, she remembers. This is beyond her.

"Captain Bascomb," Manda calls.

"Go ahead, Manda. What's going on down there?"

"Looks like we got another one of those things. This one is alive, hanging in the net."

"First mate Kotaama is on his way. Get everyone away from that thing. Thirty feet back. Get Mateo away, too. But don't tell 'em why. Just get 'em back."

"Yes, sir." She turns to them, striving for a command voice. "Okay, guys, let's all move back from the net. Captain says to back off."

"But what about that thing!" Lucas yells. "Why are we backing off! What are you going to do?"

She grabs his arm, her anger rising. "You gotta cool it, bro. Just do what I say, please." It is a familiar anger, felt often at him in the past, even as children, when he would go off, lose it, start screaming and flailing. As an adult she mastered her anger at him, internalizing finally that it only made things worse. Yet it has been months since this internal struggle last arose.

She turns him, urging him up the gangway. "Captain's orders, Lucas."

"Kotaama's on his way," she says to them all. She waves up at Mateo. "You, too, amigo. Get back from that thing."

He nods and moves away on the cross-ramp.

First Mate Kotaama appears, moving down the gangway, face dark and determined.

"Give me your pole, Lucas." He jerks Lucas's pole from his grasp and moves past them down the ramp. Lukas stands silent for once, mouth agape.

"Manda, where is this thing?" Kotaama says.

She points to the net, where the creature moves from cable to cable, its many tentacles flowing and grasping.

"You must move back with the others," he says to her.

A reanimated Lucas slips and skids after him along the gangway. Allenby, friends with Lucas, is close behind. "Sir," Lucas calls, "First mate...we gotta do something about that thing. We gotta catch it, show it to somebody. That's no fish."

Kotaama turns and points back up the gangway. "Go back with the group, Lucas, both of you. Immediately." He has an air of authority, Manda is reminded, a no-nonsense presence.

The thing has crept too high for Kotaama's pole. He waves at Mateo. "Señor, knock that thing off the net. Rapidemente. Silas, give him a hand."

Mateo steps forward, whacking at the thing with his pole. He is a heavy man but agile. The thing climbs quickly away. Silas moves to the other side of the cross ramp, pole held high. He flails at it as it moves closer, ten feet above him.

The thing jumps to Silas's pole, staggering him backwards with its sudden weight. "What the fuck!" he yells, glancing toward Kotaama on the gangway below.

"Throw your pole overboard," the Makah yells. The thing creeps down the pole towards Silas, who is suddenly pale, panicked.

"Silas, throw it in the water," Manda yells, fear replacing her anger. The smell of it is stifling, like something burnt and malevolent.

Mateo drops his own pole and moves quickly to Silas, yelling in Spanish. He wrenches the pole away and throws it. As it cartwheels over the side the thing drops off and lands on the far belt.

Kotaama yells something in his language, a curse no doubt, and vaults onto the middle belt, pole in hand. He stands and takes a swing at it across the gangway. He misses, then takes another.

From the cross ramp above Mateo retrieves his pole and spears the thing, then throws the pole and creature into the ocean. Dark liquid spills from it onto the belt. As it splashes down a cloud of steam rises. Mateo's pole beats the surface as thing writhes, tentacles grappling with it, trying to free itself.

Kotaama leaps across the gangway ramp to the far belt. Pole still in hand, he hammers at the creature in the water below.

Manda watches as its odd reptilian head turns. The glowing red pits seem to gaze up at its attacker. She covers her eyes as anguish grips her, a rush of horror and desolation. The horrible stench of the thing has invaded her. She hears herself cry out and turns away. She wants to run from the thing, escape. What is happening to her?

Shira touches her shoulder, startling her. She jumps back, turning and slipping on the wet gangway. "What!" she shouts, arms up, defensive. "What do you want!" She realizes her fright, her over-reaction. "I'm sorry," she mouths. A deep breath, then again, "I'm sorry. I don't know...I don't know what happened."

Shira looks about, taking in the situation, mystified.

The thing has sunk beneath the surface, dragging Mateo's pole down with it. Its dark stain dissipates in the water. Kotaama throws his pole, now contaminated, after it.

"Get a hose on that stuff right now," Kotaama shouts, pointing to the slime on the belt. "Allenby, grab that hose."

"What's happened?" Shira says. "Are you okay?"

Manda nods, panting.

"Shira Anders and Manda Goff to the bridge on the double," the Captain orders on their headsets.

"Manda, wait." Lucas approaches her, tone urgent, eyes wild, movements rushed and jerking. It is the brother she recognizes from so many past episodes, from their childhood onward, from urgent phone calls by friends, family, the police, hospital ERs.

"Did you see that! Did you see what Kotaama did!" These are not questions, they are cries of outrage, her brother at his worst, although not yet violent.

Manda slows her breathing, deep slow breaths. She has learned this to ward off her own crises. Her own emotional ferment is a lesser reflection of Lucas's: her childhood screaming fits, adult panic attacks, and years of struggling to learn to control them.

She grips his shoulders. He flinches but she hangs on. "Yes, Lucas, you're frightened and upset. I see that." Such words sometimes work, sometimes help to calm him. "I am, too. That creature was ugly, scary. I feel the same way."

"He killed it!" Lucas gasps. "He just killed it!"

"It's gone now, Lucas. It's gone away. He had to kill it. He had to get it away from the ship."

The spell cast by the creature has affected them both. She glances at the rest of the crew. Sarah stands gripping the rail on the opposite side, staring off at the sea. Silas seems in a daze, making ineffectual movements to help Allenby with the hose. Have they felt it as well?

Kotaama moves quickly past her. "Manda, you must come to the bridge," he says. "The Captain wants us."

"Lucas," she says, "why don't you go help Allenby. Go talk to him. Remember how to calm yourself? You can do it. I have to go to the bridge."

Two decks up Captain Bascomb stands pointing at a view screen. "Look at this," he says, his voice urgent. He turns to Shira. "Anders, you're the fish expert, right? This is the hull camera. What the hell are those things? You saw that one on the bow, right?"

The screen shows the underwater view forward, rising and falling with the ship's motion, the net hanging off the bow, sweeping into the depths, the sea cloudy and scattered with debris. Dark shapes of fish move about.

More shapes clutch the net cables. They come in and out of focus with the ship's motion, three more of the creatures. They climb the net, tentacles grasping and releasing. Still more approach from below, muscular bodies flexing as their tentacles propel them with coordinated wave-like motions. A column of bubbles rises from each one.

Shira shakes her head. "I don't know, Sir. I've never seen anything like that. They have tentacles but..." She gives a gesture of futility. "And all those bubbles."

"They are boiling the water around them." Kotaama says. "They are very hot."

"Hot and radioactive," Bascomb says, angry and loud. "What the hell are those things and where the hell...We gotta get outa here." He steps to the com box. "Jake, put us full astern, right now."

"Yes, Sir, and Sir, there was a radiation spike again."

"I figured. Get us moving, Jake, right now!"

"What about that net, Sir?" Manda says.

"The net, yeah, that damn net. Mateo," Bascomb calls to him. "We are leaving the area. Cut away that net away right now. You and Silas, cut that net away."

"It is a cable net, Sir," Mateo replies. "It does not cut. It will take a torch at least, and much time to cut every cable."

Manda feels the ship's backward motion begin, the deep tone of the engines. "Sir," she says, "I'm going back down there."

Bascomb nods, his face flushed. "Yes, go on."

"Captain, did you hear Mateo?" Kotaama says. "He said—"

"I heard him." Bascomb reaches again to the com box. "Okay, who's on the roller gear right now?"

"Cramer, sir," a voice replies. "I've got the roller."

"Can you reverse it, Mr. Cramer? Immediately. We have to drop that net."

"Yes, Sir, I can do that. It will take a few moments."

Emerging again on the bow, Manda see Lucas waving frantically, pointing. Two creatures climb the net. Kotaama follows her, stepping past, muttering in his language, then, "Captain Bascomb, there are more of them."

"I see 'em," Bascomb replies. "We're going to drop the net. Stand clear. Mr. Cramer!"

Lucas moves down the gangway toward the net, waving wildly. "What are they?" he yells. "We gotta catch one. We gotta find out what they are."

"Lucas," Kotaama shouts, loud over their headsets. "Get back here now. That's an order. Get away from those things."

The gap widens between the bow and the hanging net.

Manda cringes as the creatures' stench comes to her again. "Lucas," she yells, "come back. Get away from the bow!"

Overhead they hear a clanking of gears. The net jerks down a foot.

"Ready to back the roller, Captain," Cramer's voice comes to them. "It'll go fast. The tenders need to stand clear."

"Proceed," Bascomb calls. "Mr. Kotaama, get that man back from the bow."

Manda moves down the gangway, following Kotaama.

At the far end Lucas yells, "I'm gonna get one." He leaps for the net, grabbing at the cables and hauling himself up, feet searching for footholds.

"What the hell is that man doing?" Bascomb shouts. "First mate, get him back onboard. Cramer, belay that order. Do not drop the net."

Lucas grabs at the nearest creature, then screams in pain, jerking his hand back.

"Lucas, come back," Manda shouts, panic rising within her. She stands behind Kotaama at the end of the gangway.

"Lucas," Kotaama bellows, "jump in the water and swim to us." He looks about. "We must throw him a rescue ring. Captain Bascomb," he calls, "stop the ship. Cramer, do not—"

With a deafening clatter from the roller above, the net falls in a rush. The end slaps the gangway, barely missing them. Lucas disappears into the water as the heavy cables splash down over him.

Kotaama lunges for the end cable, but it slithers into the water.

"Oh, God," Manda yells. "Lucas!" Again she feels haunted, weak, helpless.

The ship's klaxon blares, the man overboard signal.

Lucas reappears, struggling beneath the layers of net. Two of the creatures approach him, steam rising around them.

Kotaama stands at the bow's edge, staring. He mutters in his language, then starts to pull off his shoes. Noticing Manda, he says, "I must help him."

"Señor." Mateo appears behind them, carrying an orange ring buoy with its rope. "Here is a ring. But where to throw?"

Kotaama takes it, but turning back there is no sign of Lucas. "I don't know..." He gestures toward the sinking net cables. "I don't know."

"Where is he?" Manda shouts. "Lucas!"

Kotaama hands the ring back to Mateo. He pauses at the edge, about to dive. "Maybe I can find him."

The dark shapes of two of the creatures crawl over the still visible cables, their odor strong.

"No," Manda hears herself say. Sudden purpose seizes her. "No, don't jump!" she shouts, grasping Kotaama, wrapping her arms around his broad torso. "Don't jump. You can't help him." She holds tight as he tries to pull away. "No, you'll only die, too. Let him go. It's too late."

THE SPUD

Gregg Sapp

Congratulations! This letter certifies that the artifact now in your possession is one hundred percent authentic, as advertised. I acknowledge that some explanation is in order regarding the circumstances by which it came into my possession. I do realize that this is a peculiar story, but I hope that this information satisfies your curiosity and reassures your confidence in this purchase. Your trust matters to me. This is the real deal, maybe even the ultimate collector's item (as the market for such things seems to go these days). Please note that I had this document notarized by Mr. Howard Mooers, a notary public in the state of Idaho.

On the afternoon of November 6th, 1973, the rock musician Frank Zappa entered the Pocatello (Idaho) Public Library. I was present that day, and I specifically recall that I was reading "Gulliver's Travels." At the time I was just a young man, working on the family farm while saving enough money to go to college. Because I am a rabid reader, I often used the library and was well-known to most of its staff. I mention these facts because I want to point out that the librarian on duty that day can also provide circumstantial validation of my claim. She and I remain close friends, despite our differences. Her name is Polly Crisp. She cannot, obviously, verify every detail that I claim, although she can provide witness to the general sequence of events. Note that she has signed this letter as a witness.

I recognized Mr. Zappa immediately. I was not, at that time, a particular "fan" of his music, for as I was to learn it is an acquired taste. Still, even though I had just a passing familiarity with Mr. Zappa's work, I knew very well what he looked like; for, indeed, he had one of those images that was unmistakable, with his unruly black hair falling over his shoulders, his wiry eyelashes and bushy brows, a mustache that looked like a small mammal, and that pillow of fur beneath his lip. There was nobody else in the world that looked like Frank Zappa. His unusual looks attracted general attention amongst library users, but he seemed unaffected by the gawking. If there was anybody else who might have known of Mr. Zappa, I figured that it would be an educated young woman like Polly Crisp, so I tugged on her sleeve and pointed him out to her. She nodded and whispered, "Yes, now that you mention it: that is indeed Frank Zappa."

I admit to having been a bit star struck. What on Earth was he doing in the Pocatello Public Library? I shushed a farmer who saw him and complained "What's that goddamned hippie doing here?" In my opinion, a celebrity is entitled to be eccentric. Frank Zappa went to the reference section and took down three volumes of the "Encyclopedia of Philosophy." He sat at a carrel along the wall, where he had some privacy. I watched him skimming pages rapidly, pausing to jot down occasional notes into a 3"x5" spiral notebook. When he closed the third volume and leaned back in his chair, I thought that it was a propitious moment to accost him. "Excuse me, Mr. Zappa?" I asked.

He grimaced. I realized that, being a famous rock star, he was probably approached like this everywhere he went, so I didn't take it personally that he looked me over with an annoyed expression. "So?" he replied.

I offered him a ballpoint pen and my marbled composition pad. "Could I trouble you for your autograph?" I asked.

His breath smelled of cigarettes when he said—factually, not impolitely, "I don't do autographs for simpletons."

I felt slighted, until I learned, later, that he truly did not do autographs, as a general rule. Embarrassed, I looked for a place to escape, and sought refuge in the men's room. One of the two stalls had a sign taped to the door, "Do Not Use." I went into the other and hid.

While I was sitting there, the restroom door swung open with a whoosh, and a pair of thumping footsteps entered. Peering through the crack between the stall door and the side panel, I could see a slice of Frank Zappa's face, with his lips pursed and his cheeks inflated, as he stood in front of the "Do Not Use" stall. He made a squealing sound that descended from his throat into his stomach. After a momentary pause, he ripped down the "Do Not Use" sign and went in.

I felt chagrined that I was occupying the only working toilet stall when, judging from his panting and grunting, he had a greater need than me. I was, further, absolutely mortified to think that, perhaps, he'd seen me enter the men's room and knew that it was me sitting in the stall next door. I resolved that I would stay put until after he was gone. Thankfully, that didn't take long. He sighed in deep relief and rolled the toilet paper to the ground. I heard him zipping and tucking his clothing. Last of all, he fidgeted with the toilet handle, more than once, but there was no flush. I imagined him standing there and wondering what to do, until finally he just left.

I want to state that what I did next was not at all meant to be prurient or perverse or scatological in any way! In fact, my intent was to try to flush the toilet for him. I clutched the handle; it was loose and didn't catch, but when I leaned forward to inspect it, I honestly couldn't help but see, floating, surrounded by toilet paper like in a bed of cotton, "it." It was firm and compact, a solid lump the shape of a perfect Idaho Russet potato, which I mention not because it amuses me or pleases me, but because I want to be quite clear that if its condition had been at all disagreeable, I never would have fetched it. I admit that even now, after twenty years of keeping it, I am still somewhat at a loss to explain the impulse that struck me at that moment. After he'd used the toilet, Mr. Zappa had torn aside a plastic grocery bag that was taped over the handle to discourage use and discarded it onto the floor. Reaching my hand into the bag, the way a dog owner cleans up after his animal, I retrieved the artifact. I carried the plastic bag by its handles when I left the men's room.

I was grateful when I exited the restroom to find that Frank Zappa had departed the premises. I too left in some haste, although not before being noticed by Polly Crisp, who, as I stated previously, is my witness.

That is the story of how I obtained this item. This happened almost twenty years ago. Since that time, it has remained vacuum wrapped and frozen in my cellar. Times being what they are, and with memorabilia of Mr. Zappa now being in huge demand from fans mourning his recent, untimely death, I decided to place the artifact into an online auction. I should mention to you that yours was far from the only serious offer that I received. What impressed me most favorably was that you signed your inquiry "The Greatest Frank Zappa Fan in the Galaxy." I respect your motives, as I hope that you respect mine.

Sincerely,   Witnessed by:

Joe Cletus Duke   Ms. Polly Crisp

Polly never actually saw the merchandise in question. When Joe Cletus approached the reference desk, bag in hand, he was eager to tell somebody about the trophy that he'd just collected. He did even have to say it, not in so many words.

"Guess what I have in this bag," he proffered.

Polly wrinkled her brow over a slight smile. Joe Cletus was in her Great Books Reading Group (they were reading Gulliver's Travels), and she seemed pleased, as if she fancied that he'd gotten her an-apple-for-the-teacher, or some thoughtful token of his appreciation.

"I'm sure that I couldn't guess," she replied.

Not until that moment did it occur to Joe Cletus how a proper lady like Polly might be repulsed by his acquisition. "It's a memento, sort of... something like a souvenir, or not exactly that but, uh, a keepsake, well, more like a..." A turd in a plastic bag, he mentally finished his sentence.

"What the...? Where were you? Was he in there with you?"

Joe Cletus moved the hand which held the bag behind his back.

Polly's cheeks drooped and she turned greenish, "What's in that bag?!?"

Never a liar, Joe Cletus opted for silence, and to Polly that confirmed her most vulgar suspicions.

"That's so disgusting," she wrenched her jaws as if holding back the urge to vomit.

"It isn't like, bad. He's a big rock star, famous. We don't get many famous people hereabouts."

"Oh, gee whiz! What did you do? No, don't tell me. Whatever it is, it is unhealthy, unhygienic, probably full of germs and bacteria and parasites, dangerous drugs, and who knows what else. The only decent thing that you can do with that, that, that... well, you know what, is to dispose of it."

"I'm sorry, so sorry, so very sorry. But it isn't what you're thinking. He was Frank Zappa, gosh darn it. Some people say he's a musical genius. He's considered avant-garde."

"So, do you think that makes what you did okay? It is filthy and immoral."

Filthy, he might grant her, but Joe Cletus couldn't grasp quite how it was immoral. Polly was an enigmatic authority on the subject or morality. She wasn't active in any church, although she wore a cross necklace and drove a car with a "What Would Jesus Do?" bumper sticker. She had the high, smooth forehead and soft, round eyes that Joe Cletus associated with purity of thought. Her virtuous comportment made it difficult for Joe Cletus to believe any of the things that Cowboy Burt Blackfoot claimed that Polly Crisp did back when she was the slut of Idaho Falls High School, but they were intriguing to contemplate, nevertheless.

"I'm sorry that you feel that way."

"Just get rid of it, now."

Joe Cletus twisted the bag's handles around his wrist and returned to the restroom. Once inside, though, instead of disposing of it, Joe Cletus rolled the bag like a burrito and gently stuffed it into the pocket of his jacket. When he emerged from the restroom, he showed Polly his empty hands—she nodded in acknowledgement—and proceeded out the door, straight home, where he packaged, sealed, and stored the artifact in a manner to preserve it until he figured out what to do with it.

Joe Cletus didn't seem as prepared for Polly's next reading group meeting as he normally was. She had come to count of him for a reliable ice-breaking comment, when otherwise the group sulked in silence. Eager to please, he often rescued her when she raised a question involving symbolism or rhetorical devices—usually with a wrong answer, but that was better than none. The reading group was smaller group than she'd have liked—a dozen, more or less, depending on turnout—but, instead of encouraging honesty like she hoped, the size of the group made people more self-conscious, as if each individual was keeping score on whose turn it was to talk. Polly tried to lead them as much as possible without putting words in their mouths.

"What is Gulliver's attitude toward the Lilliputians?" was her current inquiry.

Most in the group began flipping through pages in their books, pretending to be looking for some salient passage but, in reality (and Polly knew it) putting up a diversion to avoid being called upon. It was in moments like this that Polly depended on Joe Cletus. That night, though, he sat in the too small desk-and-chair, with the book closed in front of him, his face blank. Polly couldn't intercept his gaze even by walking directly in front of him. Finally, feeling a flush rising in her cheeks, she called him out.

"What's your opinion, Joseph?"

Joe Cletus stood. "I wonder why he cared so much what they thought about him."

"Yeah," Cowboy Burt Blackfoot agreed. "If I had been a giant like Gulliver, I'd have made myself king."

Polly rolled her eyes. The theme for the reading group was, "High Seas and Untamed Wildernesses: Great Adventure Novels." It proved to be less popular than her previous groups, "Happy Trails: The Literature of the American West" and "Boo! Classic Horror Stories for Adults." Those themes had been dictated to her by Howard Mooers, the pencil-thin mustachioed director of the library, who promised her that if she did well with them, he would allow her to pick the books for the next discussion group. One of them was Gulliver's Travels (abridged edition), and she was pleasantly surprised when Howard consented (she doubted that he ever actually read it), because it represented, for her, a welcome departure from the formula bestsellers and genre literature, as well as a hoped-for elevation in the quality of the material. It satisfied her immensely to enlighten the group that this book was a satire, and she advised them that they'd appreciate it more if they kept in mind that it could be read at more than one level. This was why she became a librarian in the first place, to employ the tools of her profession to help people enrich their own lives. It uplifted her to contribute to their self-actuation. That's why it stung her whenever folks seemed so clueless when she tried to start a discussion.

"Yes, but... Gulliver cooperated with the Lilliputians. Why do you think that he did that?" Polly asked, trying to regain control over the proceedings.

"To observe them," Millie Bourg chimed in.

"Yes!" Polly exalted. "And what are some of the things about them that he observed?"

"How they lived."

"Good. And what about their lives did he find so fascinating?"

Millie Bourg seemed uncomfortable answering so many questions in a row. "How little they were?"

Lucille Rader, who worked at the laundromat, contested: "No, he thought they were crazy—that whole business about cracking eggs and whichever end was right. What was that all about?"

"What was that all about?" Polly seized the opening.

The room fell silent with labored thinking. Polly ardently wished for a volunteer to attempt some amateur literary criticism, going out onto what she called a "metaphorical limb." The members of the group were timid tree-climbers, though. After a ten-Mississippi count of increasingly awkward silence, she began to wonder whether it would be better to simply tell them what to think. She thus gasped in relief when Joe Cletus raised his hand.

"Joseph?"

Joe Cletus wiped his brow with a bandana. "I still don't get why Gulliver cared what the Lilliputians thought about him."

At the University of Idaho, Joe Cletus majored in agriculture, where he learned about fertilizers for improving tuber root production and biological controls of the potato moth, among other practical things. He also became a great fan of the music of Frank Zappa. To the irritation of his roommate, Roland "Rollie" Oboler, he played Zappa constantly, Hot Rats, Weasel Ripped My Flesh, Apostrophe, Overnight Sensation, Zoot Allures, and other tasty bits that just had to be played at an obscenely loud volume. Rollie Oboler was a naïve, spud-fed Mormon lad, son of a bishop, from Arco, Idaho, with plans of going straight through to law school at UI and becoming a family practice lawyer. He self-characterized his musical interests as "easy listening," which categorically excluded Zappa.

"Turn in down!" Rollie often implored Joe Cletus, who took secret delight in exposing Rollie to some of the more scurrilous lyrics, like the part in "Dynamo Humm" where he sang about whipping off her bloomers, stiffening his thumb, and applying rotation to her sugar plum.

"What's it mean?" Rollie asked.

"Use your imagination," Joe Cletus replied. He enjoyed being thought of as a bohemian, a nonconformist, and a libertine, even if it was only in Rollie's eyes.

Apart from their divergence in musical tastes, Joe Cletus and Rollie became friends, referring to themselves facetiously as the "odd couple." Because they were seen together so often and neither had a girlfriend, many of their dormmates assumed they must be gay. They went to Vandals football games together. They studied together at a two-person table in the library. In inclement weather, they walked across the quad under the same umbrella. They dined together in the cafeteria, often sharing dessert. Neither was aware of their reputed sexual orientation until an incident following the campus jazz festival, when Joe Cletus and Rollie were accompanied back to their room by a very drunk Brady Cooper from Sigma Chi. Joe Cletus played Zappa's jazziest selection, The Grand Wazoo, and cranked up the volume.

"Let's have us a cock party!" Brady howled, unbuckling his belt.

"The bathroom is down the hall," Rollie helpfully suggested.

Joe Cletus thought it odd when Brady locked the door behind them. But when he dropped his jeans to reveal a pair of flowered bikini BVDs, Joe Cletus experienced an abrupt, train-wreck of a revelation. "Whoa, there now!" he shouted in genuine panic.

Dumbfounded, Rollie covered his eyes, but peeked between his fingers while Brady's briefs expanded.

"I thought that you dudes liked to party," Brady protested.

Meanwhile, Zappa was singing lyrics about some unknown leakage and strangers in the back seat of his car.

Fortunately, Brady projectile vomited all over Joe Cletus's turntable, which totally changed the mood of the evening. This triggered Rollie's maternal instincts; he began cleaning Brady's face, wrapping him in a large towel, and arranging for him to sleep on a sofa in the dorm lounge. By morning, all parties claimed lapses of memory. Rollie and Joe Cletus never spoke of the event, nor did Joe Cletus ever play The Grand Wazoo again for many years, unwilling to tempt its ability to release awkward memories.

The incident that never occurred nevertheless confirmed to Joe Cletus that he needed to bolster his heterosexual credentials. Anecdotally, he had heard that the local Moscow girls at the roller rink were eager for any liaison with a college man, so he cruised the area. It proved not as easy to hook up with a local girl as he'd been led to believe, but he finally realized that if he offered booze, lowered his standards, and disregarded the inner voice that warned of "jailbait," he could, in fact, succeed in that market. When he finally managed to cajole a spritely, gum-chewing local vixen back to his room, he made sure that everybody in the dormitory, especially Rollie, knew it. That night, Joe Cletus lost his virginity to a girl named Mindy, while listening to Zappa play "Black Napkins."

Joe Cletus and Mindy dated for a couple of months. Rollie didn't like her and warned that she was "Trouble with a capital T." Although Joe Cletus defended her honor and virtue, he was secretly gratified to be associated with a scarlet woman. She was his Suzy Creamcheese. Ultimately, she dumped him for a biker.

After graduating cum laude, Joe Cletus returned to the family spud farm, where since the old man wanted to retire and his older brothers had no interest whatsoever in farming, it defaulted upon him to take over operations. Folks assumed that he would fail; even the Old Man complained that a measly 300 acres family potato farm couldn't possibly survive in this age of industrial robotic agribusiness. Joe Cletus had learned a thing or two in college, though. The first thing he did was join a growers' cooperative, which operated its own packaging and distribution facility. He marketed his brand as "Zap Spuds," which people seemed to like. He used the scientific crop management techniques he learned at UI, so that he knew when, exactly, after vine kill to harvest and how to monitor hydration and pulp temperature to minimize bruising. His minor studies in business paid off, too, and he amazed the family with his forecast spreadsheets.

Above all, though, Joe Cletus was just simply a fine farmer in the old-fashioned mode of possessing a knack for nursing botanical life through healthy growth. All season long, whenever he could excuse himself for indulging in idle time, he liked to walk the rows of his field, basking in the vitality of living tubers under his feet. He loved them like his children.

Another thing that he loved about being a farmer was riding in the cab of his Spudnik tractor while motoring along to Uncle Meat or Chunga's Revenge or Waka/Jawaka or Joe's Garage all day long. He liked the image of himself as a hard-rocking radical philosopher potato farmer.

"That's nothing but noise," Cowboy Burt would complain. Annually, Joe Cletus hired him to work the conveyor during harvest, and annually he made the same comment.

"That's sophisticated music," Joe Cletus countered.

"What's so sophisticated 'bout some dude singin' about how it hurts when he pisses?" he asked.

Joe Cletus answered by turning up the volume and singing along. He knew that Cowboy Burt was as clueless about Frank Zappa as he was about treating unsprouted tubers with Gibberellic acid. Such were the spoils of Joe Cletus's higher education.

When Polly Crisp reconstituted the Great Books Reading Group, she was pleased when Joe Cletus immediately came back. Most of the previous group members returned, along with a few newcomers that Polly had actively recruited. One whom she definitely did not recruit, though, was Suzanne Havarti, the new library volunteer. Suzanne dressed like no other middle-aged woman in Pocatello. The polyester purple pants suit that she wore at the first group's meeting was skintight and showed visible undergarment lines. Her shiny heeled boots had zippers on both sides and pointed toes. When she spoke directly to somebody, she'd lean so close into that person's space that her perfume could make eyes water. Recently divorced, she had just moved to town from Missoula with all of her possessions and her four cats. When Howard Mooers asked her why she wanted to volunteer at the library, she'd replied, "Because I love books," which was the same answer that virtually everybody gave, except that when she said it, her breasts bounced so much that Howard couldn't say too quickly, "When can you start?"

At the first Great Books meeting, Suzanne Havarti and Joe Cletus arrived at the same time and sat side-by-side; Polly wasn't sure if they'd come together.

The theme was "The Great American Novel," and the first book was The Adventures of Huckleberry Finn by Mark Twain, which Polly said was, in her humble opinion, one of the greatest books ever written. Joe Cletus was surprised that she had such gushing praise for it, because he thought it was a book for adolescent boys. Still, he agreed to give it a try and, once he was a couple of chapters into it, his opinion changed—he said it was depressing.

Specifically, he shared with the group that, "It seems like everybody that Huck meets is a drunk, a crook, or a fake."

"Except Jim," Millie Bourg objected. "He is genuine."

"D'ya mean Nigger Jim?" Cowboy Burt blurted out, clearly enjoying having articulated that word out loud. Millie Bourg and Lucille Rader gasped audibly. Howard Mooers, who happened to be passing the room, stopped and scowled. "What?" Burt asked innocently. "That's what Huck calls him."

"I still don't think that you say that word," Lucille Rader insisted. "Society has evolved since those days.

"Ain't nobody prejudiced in Pocatello," Burt contended, "because everybody here is white."

The reading group laughed, but Polly was not amused. Joe Cletus intervened, "The word itself isn't prejudiced, unless it's spoken by somebody who is."

Polly applauded with relief. "That's very well put, Joseph. And I think that if Mark Twain were here right now, that's what he'd say, too."

At the end of the session, Joe Cletus got up at the same time as Suzanne Havarti; he helped her into her suede jacket. While Millie Bourg and Lucille Rader barraged Polly with questions, she watched Joe Cletus and Suzanne Havarti walking toward the door brushing hips. Impulsively, she called out "Joseph! Wait!"

The urgency in her voice froze Joe Cletus at the knees. He turned his head, while Suzanne Havarti waited in the doorway. "Yes?"

With half of the group still milling around, Polly took a long breath and hoped that by the time she exhaled, she'd have thought of something to say. "Could I have a word with you, please?" she asked.

Joe Cletus pointed at himself and raised his eyebrows. "Well..." he ruminated. "Yeah, sure."

Suzanne Havarti's heels tapped as she walked away, and by the time that Joe Cletus had turned to wish her good night, the door was swinging shut behind her.

"Would you like to have a cup of coffee with me?" Polly asked.

Joe Cletus and Polly went to U.S. Bert's Coffee Shop, where Joe Cletus had never been, but the barista knew Polly by name. There was a graying hirsute woman dressed in layers of wool, sitting alone in a corner booth, and staring into an open notebook while nibbling on a pencil. Polly pointed her out and said, "that's Gwendolyn Montana; she's a great poet." Joe Cletus wasn't sure how to order a regular cup of coffee, for the menu included foreign-sounding things like "Frappuccino" and "macchiato." Acting on his behalf, Polly requested two "grande café' Americanos," then when Joe Cletus removed his wallet, she insisted on paying.

Polly took a tattered paperback of Huckleberry Finn out of her overstuffed bag. "Do you know my very favorite passage in this book?" She didn't wait for him to answer before, reaching across for his hand, she put his finger on it. "Read this," she urged, placing her hand on his thigh.

Joe Cletus cleared his throat as if he speaking to an audience. "I was a- trembling, because I'd got to decide, forever, betwixt two things, and I knowed it. I studied a minute, sort of holding my breath, and then says to myself: All right then, I'll go to hell."

Grinning expectantly, Polly waited for a reaction.

"It's interesting" he said.

"It is, isn't it! To me, it means that doing the right thing is worth any consequence. What's does it mean to you?"

Joe Cletus scratched his head. "I'm not sure that Huck meant it literally."

"Of course not. Mark Twain was an atheist. He didn't believe in hell."

"You don't say."

"Most people have an entirely wrong impression of Mark Twain, like he is everybody's weird uncle. But he could be abusively sarcastic. He didn't seem to care what other people thought about him."

"How could anybody not care about that?" Joe Cletus pondered.

Although Polly knew that Joe Cletus had a college degree and was unusually well spoken for a potato farmer, she'd never thought of him as a particularly well-read person. Most of the books that he checked out of the library were about soils or heavy equipment repair. Still, when she asked him what he read, for pleasure, she was impressed to learn that at his personal summer project was to read Moby Dick. This inspired her to ask Joe Cletus if he cared to suggest future themes for the reading group.

"I got a suggestion. I bet you'll never guess."

"Science fiction?"

"No."

"Mysteries?"

Joe Cletus shook his head. "Nah. Ain't even close. How about, like, I call them hippie novels?"

"What do you mean?"

"It's kind of weird, but I like reading things that stretch your head, kind of loopy stories by writers like Tom Robbins and Ken Kesey and Donald Barthelme and Kurt Vonnegut and, well, guess what I'm reading right now..."

"What?"

"The Hitchhiker's Guide to the Galaxy."

"Well, I'm impressed," Polly declared, making a mental note to see if the library had that book. She patted her hand on Joe Cletus's lap. "Well, well... I guess that I shouldn't be surprised. You have diverse tastes. Like your fondness for that rock star who once came to the library,"

"Frank Zappa!"

"Of course; he's with that group the Mothers of Convention, right?"

"Invention. Mothers of Invention. They're avant-garde." Polly thought that Joe Cletus was trying to impress her, then he ruined the moment by boasting, "I have a souvenir of his visit to Pocatello at home, in the freezer..."

Polly felt her cheeks turn to stone. On the guise of checking her wristwatch, she removed her hand from his lap. "It is getting late... and, well, it's been an interesting evening, Joseph."

"Yes, it has."

Polly flashed a mental image of Joe Cletus impulsively pulling her across the table, into his face, and kissing her hard enough to distract her from what she didn't want to think about.

"Goodnight, then. See you at the group, next week," she said.

After that, Joe Cletus stopped going to the group. Every week, Polly waited until well after the hour before starting, in case he was running late. She wondered if she called him to ask him to come back, would he?

One year, Roland Obobler came to town for a bar association meeting, and he brought his whole family and his pregnant wife with him. Four kids in eight years, and another on the way. He looked middle aged; his unblemished brow was now creased, and that comb-over the bald terrain of his head evidenced a vanity that Joe Cletus had never suspected in him. Time and, perhaps, practicing the law seemed to have changed him, because whereas he used to be pristine in his behavior and capable of speaking no words harsher than "mercy me," he now cracked his knuckles, picked his nose, and used non-canonical curse words like "friggin'" and "shee-at."

Joe Cletus asked him what kind of law he practiced; Roland replied: "I'm part of a team; we call ourselves The Ultimate Defenders. We take personal injury and workers' compensation cases. You might've seen our commercial if you've ever watched TV in Boise. It's really cool; the three of us partners wear camouflage and eye black as we walk away from a courtroom with smoke and burning fire behind us. Our motto is: We'll Go to War for Your Rights. Business is booming!"

Joe Cletus had seen that commercial but failed to recognize Roland in it, and even now he still couldn't identify which of the three soldiers in battle gear was him. "These days, it seems like everybody wants to sue somebody," he said non-judgmentally.

"It's the American way."

On the first night that Roland Oboler was in town, Joe Cletus accepted an invitation to go out to dinner with him and his wife, while the au pair girl that they travelled with watched the kids in the hotel room. Ursula Oboler, Roland's wife, was chubby, with blotted lipstick and flaming red hair wound in pig tails. She unabashedly invited Joe Cletus to rub her belly to induce the baby inside to kick. She said, "It's great to meet one of Rollie's old friends," and begged Joe Cletus that "If you have any funny stories about my hubby's college days, I'm all ears."

Rollie made a slicing gesture against his throat to stifle Joe Cletus, who happened at that moment to recall the incident with Brady Cooper.

They had a nice dinner at the Sandpiper, after which Ursula excused herself so that, "You boys can talk about old times."

"Yeah. Hey Joe Cletus, I'd love to see that farm you were always bragging about."

Joe Cletus and Rollie hopped into the pickup truck and drove outside of town, to the fertile 300 acres where the world's tastiest potatoes were grown. Given any opportunity, Joe Cletus was always anxious to accept visitors on the farm, since he was proud of how straight his rows were and seldom got a chance to show them off. After a jarring ramble over the dirt service road, a stop in the barn to examine the heavy equipment and feed the llamas, and a brief digression where Joe Cletus enlisted his friend's help to rotate the wheel line, Rollie held up his greasy palms and showed them proudly to Joe Cletus. "That's hard work," he grunted. "Buddy, you got anything cold to drink?"

"Got some iced tea back at the house." He then paused and asked, "Is tea okay for you to drink?"

At this, Rollie nearly split his gut laughing. "How about a cold beer?"

"Beer?" Joe Cletus.

"The colder the better."

Thinking about it, Joe Cletus recalled that he kept a six pack of Coors Light in the cellar for whenever his father visited. "Sure," he said, pleased at the idea of having a beer-drinking guest. Although Joe Cletus apologized for the clutter of newspapers, magazines, discarded clothing, dirty dishes, and assorted spills and piles, Rollie just cleared a space on the couch and sat down. He was grinning like somebody who was getting away with something that he knew was wrong. Joe Cletus fetched the entire six pack and placed it on a table between them. Rollie took a healthy, wide-mouthed gulp that made his Adam's apple bob.

"This is the life, eh?" Rollie remarked. "Do you know what'd be cool, right now? Do you still own any of that crazy old Frank Zappa music that you used to play all of the time?"

There were over 20 Zappa LPs, 30 CDs, and a dozen or so cassette or 8-track tapes in Joe Cletus's collection. From that selection, he chose the live album, Tinseltown Rebellion, turning up the volume so that Zappa's "Panty Rap" narration could be heard. Rollie exalted with a thumbs-up and, when he heard the words "feminine underclothing," he hooted out loud, "That's so sick it's almost funny."

Joe Cletus finished a beer, which gave him a great idea. "Do you want to know what else is so sick it is almost funny?"

"Yeah."

"Wait right here," he instructed Rollie, who was too moved by the hilarity of the "Panty Rap" to do otherwise. Joe Cletus scrambled downstairs into the cellar. The freezer was totally empty except for a bag of ice, a rack of venison, and a vacuum wrapped, labeled, and dated package, which contained a perfect celebrity turd.

"Catch," Joe Cletus called out, tossing the package to Rollie.

His instincts impaired, Rollie was unable to react quickly enough to catch it, so it bounced off his ribs into his lap. "What th' hell?"

In the background, Frank Zappa was rapping, Underpants, brassieres, just send 'em up, no problem.

Roland lifted the package by its ends and blew on it to see through the frost. "What's this? Some kind of spud?" He squeezed it. "Wait just one minute...?!?"

"It's from Frank Zappa himself," Joe Cletus confirmed, expecting a good laugh and maybe a fist bump. "Genuine doo doo."

Leaping bolt upright as if electroshocked, Rollie simultaneously clutched his heart, and, wiping his mouth with his sleeve, slurred, "Gee whiz, Joe Cletus, what kind of a sicko are you?"

From fall, 1989 to early 1990, Polly was "unwell," as Howard Mooers explained her extended leave of absence. She'd begun to exhibit uncharacteristic behaviors that stimulated rampant gossip among the community of regular library patrons. One afternoon Millie Bourg saw Polly leaving the Center Street Tavern, and not walking very straight, either. Upon sharing this information with Lucille Rader, they began to keep an eye on her during Great Books Discussion Group meetings, and, upon confirmation from Cowboy Burt, they agreed that one night her speech was slurred, and her breath smelled like peppermint schnapps. Shamelessly, Cowboy Burt exploited her condition by inviting her to shoot pool with him at the tavern afterwards. Several people noticed his pickup truck parked outside of her duplex the next day. This "unwell" behavior deteriorated, involving more escapades with Cowboy Burt and bottles of liqueur, until one night she did not report for a meeting of the

Great Books Reading Group. Millie Bourg and Lucille Rader later intimated to Joe Cletus that they heard that Polly checked herself into "rehab."

Then, in February while the fields were frozen and Joe Cletus usually took a couple of weeks off in Arizona, Polly returned. When he saw the flyers that she posted in the grocery store announcing that the Great Books Reading Group was being re-re-formed, Joe Cletus wasn't sure if he was interested, but even so he cancelled his pilgrimage to Sedona. Polly promoted the new group tirelessly, at schools, civic associations, nursing homes—wherever she thought that she could find potential readers. Her restored enthusiasm mirrored her new spirituality, for after all those years of countless knocks on the door from elders and well-intentioned neighbors, Polly finally converted to Mormonism. Her religious zeal was reflected in the theme that she selected for the new Reading Group, "Tales of Hope and Inspiration."

Joe Cletus was ambivalent about whether to commit to another reading group. He was one of the first persons in Pocatello to subscribe to dial-up Internet access at his farm, and ever since he'd been spending less and less time reading, and more time "riding" (not "surfing") the Web. Then, by chance, he bumped into Polly in the ten-items-or-less checkout line at Albertson's, and before he could say "hi," she was raving about how great it was to see him again.

"You've gained weight," Joe Cletus observed.

"I feel fantastic!" she chirped. "You're coming to the next Great Books meeting, right?"

She seemed a little too perky for somebody who'd recently been "unwell." Joe Cletus was afraid that to say something that might trigger a relapse, so he promised her, "Yeah, I wouldn't miss it."

Despite Polly's ardent recruitment efforts, the re-re-constituted group consisted of the same regulars from before, including Suzanne Mooers (previously Havarti), and half a dozen old-timers bussed in from the Mount Moriah retirement home. Undaunted, Polly welcomed them "from the bottom of my heart." The book under discussion was The Little Prince.

"Okay, group. This wonderful book is the parable of the Little Prince, who lives on his very own asteroid and loves a rose that he fears does not return his love. So, feeling lonely and betrayed, he flies away to visit other worlds. What is he searching for?"

Was this a trick question? She already said he wanted to be loved. Still, there were no immediate volunteers to answer. Joe Cletus knew that Polly was looking right at him, although he kept his head down.

"Maybe he needs to see what's out there," Suzanne Mooers finally proposed.

"His asteroid wasn't big enough for him," Millie Bourg suggested.

"There were things he wanted to experience in life," Lucille Rader proposed.

"Or he just had to sow his wild oats," Cowboy Burt countered.

The members advanced a couple additional interpretations, all without comment from Polly, until the chattering died down and the group looked to her for the correct answer. If she knew it, though, she wasn't telling.

Unable to endure the silence any longer, Joe Cletus stood when he spoke. "If he hadn't flown off, there'd be no book."

Millie Bourg and Lucille Rader exchanged uncertain glances. Cowboy Burt asked, "Huh?" Even Polly seemed dubious, and she never questioned his answers. Her face became flushed, her cheeks drooped, and she hastened to grab a tissue to dab her eyes before tears had a chance to trickle down.

Frank Zappa died on December 4th, 1993, at the age of 53. The prostate cancer that killed him was already advanced and inoperable by the time of its diagnosis. For several months before his demise, Zappa was alert and occupied with his music, even though he knew that he was rapidly dying. In a May 1993 interview on the Today Show, he was asked how he wanted his legacy to be remembered. Without hesitation, he replied, "It's not important to even be remembered."

On the day that Frank Zappa died, Joe Cletus spent the whole afternoon driving his Spudnik back and forth across frozen fields, listening to both CDs of Shut Up and Play Your Guitar. He pulled over and wept into his gloves when he heard "Black Napkins." That night, by the gray light of his computer, he continued paying homage to Zappa by playing all three CDs of Lather from start to finish while commiserating with true believers on various rock-oriented electronic discussion lists. He corresponded extensively with somebody whose alias was "Disco Boy" and who claimed unequivocally to be "The greatest Frank Zappa fan in the galaxy." In support of that contention, Disco Boy enumerated the items in his collection of Zappa memorabilia: posters, t-shirts, concert tickets, tube socks, coffee mugs, guitar picks, framed album covers, a bobble head doll, a headband that he'd worn onstage at a concert in Columbus, Ohio, a training bra that was purported to have been donated during the original panty rap, and some corporeal relics including nail clippings and locks of hair. It was a mind-boggling roster of paraphernalia, but Joe Cletus knew that he could go one better...

"NO WAY!!!," Disco Boy, the galaxy's greatest Frank Zappa fan, replied when Joe Cletus told him what he had.

"Way," Joe Cletus typed back.

The cursor on the blank screen blinked interminably. Finally, Disco Boy wrote, "I have a business proposition for you."

When the Federal Express delivery man carrying a refrigerated package rang the bell at the suburban Boise home, the galaxy's Greatest Frank Zappa fan was eagerly awaiting. He'd taken the afternoon off to be there when the package arrived. There was a letter taped to the outside of the box, upon which was written "Read me first." More curious than impatient, the greatest Frank Zappa fan in the galaxy opened the letter and read it standing in the sunlit foyer of his home. He hummed. He chuckled. He felt blood throb in his temples and an expression that combined pity, amusement, and disgust stretched his cheeks and tugged the corners of his mouth.

"What a degenerate," Roland Oboler scoffed. "A real sick sicko."

TIMBER AND ITS PURPOSES

Charles Wilkinson

"If you're so interested in the Plenderleiths, why don't you invite them over for a drink?"

Gordon Baverstock ignored his wife. He was standing by the picture window and gazing down at a half-timbered house and an untended garden that ran down to the river's edge. If it were not for the humidity, it could have been autumn, not early August. For almost a fortnight, grey-flannel clouds had covered the sky, a moist morass always at the point of precipitation, but never yielding more than a sense there was rain in the air. A proper thunderstorm was needed to clear away the closeness and allow the blue to break through.

"Perhaps."

"Perhaps? Don't overdo the decisiveness, will you, dear? Something might actually happen."

He turned towards his wife. She was a small woman with pinched features and prone to periodical attacks of sarcasm. Her current complaint was that he was doing nothing with his retirement.

"If you insist."

"I don't. But perhaps making their acquaintance will cure this curious fascination you have for them. Then you can stop staring out of the window, and we can get on with our lives."

There had been two bungalows in the village when the Baverstocks arrived: their own and Margery's. The house and the nearby plot of land had been purchased by Plenderleith. Within days, the old woman's house had been demolished. Almost before the ground had settled, Plenderleith arrived with pantechnicons and builders to erect a timber-framed house. Although it had been completed with singular celerity, the house looked as if it had been there for centuries.

"Do you think that they've reassembled an old house? The tiles don't look new, do they? And neither do the timbers."

"Well, if you invite them round, you'll be able to ask them, won't you?"

A week later, Plenderleith was seated in the leather armchair to the left of the grandfather clock in the Baverstocks' living room. He was a tall man with thin white flesh so taut on his bone structure that he appeared to have been unearthed from a Viking burial mound. His eyes were pale blue and faraway. He wore shabby green trousers and a jacket of damp-looking tweed, grey but flecked with white as if impregnated with sea salt and rain. His wife, he explained, was not able to accept their invitation because of the children.

"Now, what will you have?"

Mr. Baverstock rubbed his hands together. There were canapés and crisps on the table; a regiment of spirits, ice buckets, and cocktail shakers on the sideboard.

"Water."

"Ah ... capital ... one water coming up. Ice?"

"It'll not be necessary."

Mrs. Baverstock went to the kitchen and returned with a tumbler and two bottles.

"Sparkling or still?"

Plenderleith glanced at her. "From the tap."

His abruptness was, to an extent, mitigated by his soft accent. Scottish beyond a doubt—and wasn't there an undertow of Aberdeenshire?

"I was remarking to my wife, only the other day, how well your house seems to have settled into the landscape. It bears no resemblance to a new build."

"It's an old house. With later additions."

"Ah, yes ... I thought as much. And tell me, what's your line?"

"My business? Is that what you're talking about?"

"Yes, your business."

"Timber and its purposes."

"And so, you're a merchant. A joiner?"

"Phrase it as you will. Plenderleiths have a long association with wood and water—that's for sure."

After Plenderleith left. Anthea Baverstock began to clear away. Plenderleith's plate was clean, for he had refused all offers of canapés. His glass was empty, although Mr. Baverstock could not recall him bringing it to his mouth. But what was most striking was the condition of the leather armchair. It was noticeably damp and smelt faintly of wet mud as if the man who'd occupied it had been swimming at the bottom of a stream.

* * *

The next day Baverstock took his blackthorn walking stick and went down to the riverbank. To his left, Plenderleith's children were playing: four lean little boys with bread-pale faces who were skipping into the grey water, where they would wade in the shallows for a while before rushing out. It was strange that they did this silently, the only sound being the splash of their feet as they entered the flow. A small girl, her head bowed in concentration, was alone on the grass and appeared to be painting a tiny picture on a pebble.

Now that he had a view of the rear of the house, Baverstock could see that it was larger than he'd realized. Two wings with leaded windows encroached on part of what had been Margery's overgrown garden. The ground adjacent to it had been cleared of wildflowers, thistles, and foxgloves. The patches of reddish-brown soil that had been uncovered seemed raw compared to the surrounding black and white of the building, the pallid river, and the white-grey cloud cover, so low today it was as if it might descend to bandage the raw earth. The only possible improvement to the surroundings was a sculpture in the shape of a monolith, which had been decorated with a spiral pattern. He was reminded of a conversation with his wife earlier that morning. There had been a number of break-ins in the village; strangely, nothing was ever taken. After one such intrusion, a friend of Anthea had noticed that someone had taken a knife to the beams, scoring the timber with Roman numerals and symbols, the significance of which eluded her.

"Well, the Roman numerals," Baverstock had told her, "are easy to explain. They're carpenter's marks. They were used to help the builders when the wooden skeleton of the house was being assembled."

"Then they would be medieval. These were recent."

"Perhaps she simply didn't see them before. They're not always immediately visible to the naked eye."

"She's a very observant woman. And anyway, if I can dignify it with such a term, your theory does not consider the symbols."

"No doubt there's a perfectly reasonable explanation."

Baverstock, who disliked being contradicted so soon after breakfast, had opened his newspaper, putting an end to the conversation.

Tired of their game, the children ran back in the direction of the house. Baverstock waited until they were inside before moving close to the barbed wire fence that separated Plenderleith's property from common land. Beyond the house, there were woods and, close by them, a shed that must have been recently erected. A pile of timber had been stacked next to it, the top of which was covered by a tarpaulin. Evidently, Plenderleith had purchased the woods at the same time as he'd bought Margery's bungalow. A shift in the wind direction brought in a whisper of rain. He should have taken his umbrella and not a walking stick. As he was about to turn away, he became aware of movement in the woods. Then three animals emerged from the undergrowth. It was a moment before he tentatively identified them as a breed of pig that he'd not come across before. Their snouts were unnaturally long, practically canine. He made a mental note to mention them to Anthea, who would doubtless have been able to identify them instantly.

* * *

"There's been another one," said Baverstock, coming from the front room, which overlooked the church.

"Do you think I can't hear the bells?"

They were in the first month of meteorological winter, and already there had been five funerals. Sodden summer had given way to incessant rain, flash floods, and swollen rivers. Part of what had been Margery's garden was under the water, but as far as he could discern, there was no threat to the Plenderleith's house, let alone his own property.

"It's not surprising that old people are dying. Probably an excuse to get away from this foul weather."

"They're not all elderly. I spoke to the man who lives in the cottage next to the Post Office. He's a retired doctor but still does some work at the surgery as a locum. Apparently, there's a disease going around they can't identify. When you think you've almost got over it, your lungs fill up with water, and you drown."

"Thank you for that, Anthea. Just the sort of information I require before lunch."

They bickered for the rest of the morning and most of the afternoon. Four times, Baverstock took up his blackthorn walking stick and went to the front door. The rain was remorseless: the back garden saturated, every blade of grass several shades darker; the silver birch dripping; the path down to the river reduced to a mudslide. Even the briefest of excursions would be ill-advised. Around teatime, a truce was declared.

"Do you remember I told you about a friend whose house was broken into?"

"Vaguely. That was months ago, wasn't it? A problem with the timbers, I seem to recall."

"Someone had scored the beams with Roman numerals and strange symbols."

"Ah, yes."

"Well, my friend took photographs and sent them to an acquaintance at a university. It turns out the Roman numerals do resemble carpenter's markings."

"Now, wasn't that just what I said?"

"But why would anyone wish to put carpenter's marks on a building completed centuries ago? The symbols, it's been established, are Pictish."

"If they were intended to ward off evil weather, they haven't done a very good job."

"No one knows what they mean. In most cases, you can't even make a credible guess."

"Perhaps they should ask Plenderleith. He hails from that part of the world."

At the mention of Plenderleith, the temporary ceasefire broke down. Why was Gordon so obsessed with Plenderleith? The man had never returned their hospitality. His wife was a distinctly dour woman, with her hair drawn back into a bun and a long face straight out of American Gothic. She didn't so much as glance at you in the street, let alone return your greeting. The children were feral and no more inclined to speech than their mother.

After exchanging asperities, Gordon was reduced to resentful silence and the pretense of reading his newspaper. His wife retreated into her novel. At around six o'clock, he glanced at his watch. It was the hour when they normally opened a bottle of wine, but Anthea was parading one of her periodic bouts of abstinence. The mere pop of the cork would be met with silent disapproval; a second glass would be openly derided as an attempt to undermine her hard-won sobriety.

"I'm going for a walk."

"What? In this weather?"

"It's eased off. If I'm late, leave my supper in the oven."

He slipped into the cellar and took out a bottle of wine and a corkscrew. Now was the time to pay the Plenderleiths a visit. He had the excuse of an errand to inquire about Pictish symbols. He couldn't believe that nothing was known about their meanings. And anyway, these people were his nearest neighbors. Wasn't it perfectly natural that he should drop by? There was much to be said for being on good terms with them. No doubt Plenderleith's hospitality would be Lenten at best, but perhaps Mrs. Plenderleith could be persuaded to take a glass.

Outside, blue-black clouds filtered the sunlight, trapping the landscape in counterfeit dusk. The trees, still dripping, were burdened with leaves of iron. Below him, the river had the dull gleam of amalgam. He almost slipped on the path's oily mud and decided that squelching over the sopping grass beside it was preferable. There were no lights on in Plenderleiths' house. He'd always assumed that the front door was in the façade opposite him, but now he recalled a larger entrance at the back. As he made his way around, a dark form, larger than a dog, swam into sight and then moved off silently as he approached. It was a moment before he recalled the pigs. As soon as he reached the rear of the house, he made out a yellow glow in one of the windows and the silhouettes of small people. A faint rustling and shuffling in the woods suggested the maneuvering of animals, forces massing for an unknown purpose. Now that he was near the window, the figures pressing against the panes revealed themselves as children. There was enough illumination to see that their faces and naked upper bodies were painted with long slashes of color and spirals and shapes like axes and seahorses. He gestured to them to open the door, but they continued to study him with eerie impassivity.

As he edged his way toward where he thought the entrance was, he noticed that the hut door was open, revealing a copper-colored radiance within. He changed direction, staggering for a moment on the slippery ground. Once he'd reached the hut, he stood still, listening for sounds inside. He pushed the door. It opened noiselessly. In front of him were rows of coffins. Some were varnished to a liquid gleam; others were clearly incomplete. A few had their lids off, revealing velvety interiors. Planks and saws leaned against the wall. At the far end of the room, Plenderleith was seated at a desk, his back to the door. His head was lowered as if to study invoices or orders. Baverstock returned the way he'd come, taking care not to look in the direction of the children, lest they should still be watching him from the window.

* * *

After the early morning mist lifted, the day brightened, disclosing slivers of blue between the cloud banks. At least it was no longer raining. From his position by the picture window, Baverstock noticed the grass and the path were recovering. A stray shaft of sunlight silvered the river. His wife sat at the table; her laptop open.

"We've been invited out tonight," she said, without taking her eyes off the screen.

"Oh, who by?"

"Veronica Hartnett."

"Who's she?"

"The friend I was telling you about. The one who had the break-in."

"Oh, yes. It's all a bit sudden, isn't it?"

"No, she asked us weeks ago, but I didn't want to give you time to make excuses for not going."

"So, it's a compulsory party."

"It's not really a party. It'll be just the three of us. And you're not to ruin it by rabbiting on about the Plenderleiths. In fact, as an advance reward for not mentioning them, I will tell you what their name means."

"It's Scottish, isn't it?"

"It means something like timber, farm, and river. All fairly apt, I suppose, since he told us his trade involves timber, and he lives by a river. But no farm as yet."

Baverstock recalled that he had not told her about the pigs. Neither had he mentioned the previous evening's expedition. "He keeps animals, I think. They're pig-like."

"*I think* and *pig-like.* We're a paragon of precision this morning."

"Well, they might be wild, but I certainly didn't see them before Plenderleith arrived. And they appear to be some breed of pig, possibly crossed with a dog."

"I hardly think that's likely."

Baverstock described them to her, and for once, she had the good grace to look puzzled. "I can't think what those might be. Perhaps he's imported them. Anyway, I've found out what your man does for a living."

"Oh?"

"He's an undertaker."

In a way, this was a relief. It would hardly be comforting to think that what he'd witnessed the previous evening was some kind of private hobby. "Well, he's had plenty of customers recently."

At six o'clock, Baverstock put on a jacket and tie for what turned out to be his only encounter with Veronica Hartnett, who proved an agreeable host, serving excellent canapés and a commendable claret. Anthea declared a respite from abstinence. No mention of the Plenderleiths was made during what he later described to the newspapers as a pleasant but ordinary occasion. The only link with subsequent events occurred late in the evening. Veronica explained that though the façade of her house was Georgian, it concealed a much older building. The front room in which they were sitting was Jacobean. However, the core of the house was even earlier—medieval, in all probability—and this was where the beams had been damaged. When they went through to inspect, Baverstock agreed that the addition of the carpenter's marks was undeniably of a recent date. The symbols were various. Alongside abstract shapes, animal heads were also depicted. Crudely carved into the ancient wood, the creatures concerned defied identification, although one bore some resemblance to a seahorse. What the significance of this was, no one could imagine. Veronica also confessed bewilderment that, although more than a few houses in the village had been broken into, only hers had been singled out for this treatment.

That night the Baverstocks relaxed into a wine-soaked sleep. It was not till eleven the next morning that the postman brought them the news that Veronica was dead and her house had been demolished. Over the next few hours, they pieced together the story from several sources. The owner of the Post Office confirmed that the attack was thought to have begun at around three o'clock in the morning. In the convenience store, it was reported that several people, on rushing to their bedroom windows, had seen a pack of wild animals, accompanied by half-naked children, running silently down the main street. The former doctor, who was quickly called to the scene, confided that Veronica's remains had been savaged by large dogs. The police, as always in that remote part of the country, were late to arrive. In their defense, everyone agreed the attack had been accomplished with preternatural speed.

In the days, weeks, and months that followed, more details and many rumors emerged. The house had not been entirely demolished. The front rooms were still standing. Only the oldest parts had been destroyed, reduced to a rubble of masonry mingled with wattle and daub. All the beams had been taken. The wild animals were described severally as pig-like, obviously lupine, and as creatures that bore the characteristics of both or seemed impossible to categorize.

Shortly after the incident, the pantechnicons arrived at dusk. By the next morning, Plenderleith's house had gone, leaving little more than a few pieces of mortar strewn on the ground. The whole structure appeared to have been folded and taken away as if it were no more than a tent. The hut, along with its contents, also vanished. In a dream, Baverstock saw the Plenderleiths rebuilding their house, along with a new wing made of old beams. As the owner could not be contacted, the site by the river proved impossible to sell. The wildflowers and the weeds returned to what had been Margery's garden: hawkbit, larkspur, herb robert, foxglove, and nettles.

URBAN DECAY

Wayne Kyle Spitzer

"Each of us, I think, had to understand it on our own terms, the totality of the desolation, the speed at which the old world had fallen away. Each of us, I think, had something of an epiphany looking down at it.

For me, it was seeing the helicopter's shadow slink wraith-like over the hulk-jammed freeways and overgrown downtown intersections, realizing that shadow was the only thing—the only *human* thing—moving in any direction. For Sam it may have been the aircraft carrier—the *USS Nimitz*, Roman had said—run aground between Pike Street Market and the big Ferris wheel (and presumably straight into the State Route 99 tunnel). Leastwise that's what she was looking at as she gasped audibly and the helicopter swung north by northeast, over what would have been Belltown, toward the Space Needle.

"You gotta see this," said Roman, his voice sounding generic, condensed, tinny over the headsets. "Anyone here ever seen an eagle's nest? In the wild, I mean?"

Lazaro hmphed. "I've scaled a 200-foot Douglas fir and touched one. Does that count?"

Nigel sneered—you could actually *hear* it, even from the front. "Ya, mon. But only in your dreams."

Roman nodded at Lazaro. "Yeah? Was it big?" He sounded jocular, condescending. "How big was it, you think?"

"I don't know. About four feet," said Lazaro. He seemed annoyed—even hurt. "What's it matter?"

"I was just wondering how it compared to, say, that, at five o'clock."

We all saw it at once as the helicopter leaned and I was pressed against Sam: a nest the size of one of those above-ground pools—the kind someone like Lazaro might have had before the Flashback—built up around the Needle's radio tower and comprised of mud and fallen timber.

"Jesus, it's everywhere," whispered Sam, her face and chesnut-brown hair—which smelled of honeysuckle and gunpowder—reflected in the glass. "They—they're blue, *teal.* Like robins' eggs." She shook her head pensively, meditatively. "I wouldn't have thought that."

"Where's momma bird?" said Lazaro.

"That's a good question," muttered Roman. He made a complete circuit of the Needle before leaving its orbit completely and heading back in the direction we'd come. "Nor are we sticking around to find out." His voice became suddenly focused. "Okay. I'm going to fly low between the buildings—because you can bet we're being watched. So, don't freak out. The idea is to shield our location from prying eyes for as long as possible—or at least until the chopper's up and everyone is clear. Got it?"

Check. Downtown Seattle was not a safe place, especially in the business district, and not just because there were pterodactyls roosting in the skyscrapers. For one, it bordered on territory controlled by the Skidders, a ruthless gang which operated out of Doc Maynard's Public House and Underground Tour in Pioneer Square. It also shared a border with New Beijing and a group called the Gang of Four. Neither, Roman had assured us, were to be trifled with, and both were known to make frequent excursions into the no-man's land of the business district. Throw in roving packs of velociraptors, which were also territorial, or the occasional tyrannosaurid, or even an herbivore with the Flashback in its eyes, and you had a situation which needed to be gotten into and gotten out of quickly.

And *quietly.*

"Just *stay in range,*" I said, checking the switch of my walkie-talkie, making certain it was on. "Or it'll be a shitshow all over again."

It was a cheap remark—no one had been closer to Chives than Roman—and one I regretted immediately. "No," he said, and crossed himself. "It won't. Trust me. Anything bigger than an alley cat—you're going to know it. We'll get you inside, I promise."

"It's not getting inside I'm worried about. It's getting *out* with what we came for."

He looked at me with those damned earnest eyes—something I would have preferred he didn't do, especially while thundering between skyscrapers—and smiled. "We'll do that, too. Now lock and load, Jamie. All of you. We're almost there."

"See that courtyard just east of the library? That's our landing zone," said Roman, slowing us to a near hover, beginning to lower altitude.

I watched as the helicopter's shadow grew on the wild, waving grass.

"Again: when you hit dirt, I want you to go immediately to the street—5th Avenue, right there, and follow it south-west. Stay close to the buildings, they'll give you some cover. Get ready."

"From predators?" asked Joan, our mechanic, her voice full of doubt. It was her first time out of the compound with us.

"From *people,*" said Roman. "They've been known to snipe from the towers." We touched down with a slight bounce—tall grass lashing at the windows. "Remember, right on Marion ... then all the way to 1st—to the Exchange Building. You can't miss it: there's a Starbucks across the street with a—"

Joan balked. "There must be a hundred—"

"... with a gutted triceratops in its window." He looked at her over his shoulder, then at each of us individually. "It's—it's probably been picked clean by now." He swallowed as though he'd said too much, then straightened suddenly and nodded once. "Everyone just—stay sharp, okay? Good luck."

And then we were moving, piling out of the hatch and into the prop-wash, scrambling for the street, as the Bell 206 climbed—the sound of its rotors thundering, reverberating off the buildings, the grass dancing.

"Other side of the intersection, that condo," I said, "let's go."

We double-timed across the pavement—or what was left of it—to where a concrete overhang offered some measure of cover.

"Hold up," said Nigel. He dropped to his knees and began assembling his weapon—a commercial weed trimmer outfitted with a 10" saw blade—as Lazaro hovered above him.

"Yeah, hold up. Nigel saw some grass he wants to trim," said Lazaro.

Nigel primed the trimmer but didn't start it. "I didn't hear you complain when this opened the belly of that Barney—you know the one that had you pinned? Or did you forget about that?"

"And covered me with its guts," said Lazaro. He pumped his shotgun briskly. "You were too close. Charlene would have taken you both."

"That so, mon? Like it took Chives?"

I glanced at Lazaro and saw him bunching a fist. "Stand down, Lazaro ... I said stand down! Now!" I looked at the others quickly, hoping to quell any unrest. "We all know precisely what happened to Chives ... and there ain't nothing—I mean nothing—that is going to change that. Ever." I made eye contact with Nigel as he stood. "He couldn't be left that way. Period. Now let's move—Lazaro, take point. Nigel, bring up the rear. Let's go."

And we went, hustling down 5ᵗʰ Avenue even as the sky grumbled and it began to spit rain—all the way to Marion Street, at which we turned right ... and were promptly greeted by a hail of gunfire.

At first it had seemed like a miracle, the fact that there was an underground garage opening right there and that we'd all managed to get into it before anybody was hit—at least until the metal gate came rattling down and we realized our attackers hadn't so much targeted us as *herded* us directly into a trap.

"Drop 'em, now!" came a voice, even as we spun in its direction and raised our weapons—and quickly realized there was nothing to shoot at. Nothing visible, at any rate. What there was, however, were tiny red dots—on our foreheads, over our hearts.

"You see them. Good," said the voice, just as cool as iced tea—the perfect accompaniment to the clatter of shifting firearms. "And now you're going to bend down ... slowly ... and lay all your weapons at your feet. All right? *Nooo* one has to get hurt. Just do as I say ... and then we can have a nice conversation. About who you are, for example. And where you're from. And what you're doing being dropped off by a helicopter in the middle of disputed territory. Our territory. Okay?"

"Okay," I said, and nodded at the others—and at Lazaro twice; we'd been in this situation before, and he always wanted to play chicken.

Slowly everyone did it—the red dots never wavering, the rain starting to rattle against the gate.

"Is that a *weed* whacker?" said the voice and was followed by laughter. "Damn."

I heard the tapping of what turned out to be an axe head against concrete before I realized he'd stepped into a shaft of gray light. "Don't let their laughter get to you—people used to laugh at us too."

We watched, paralyzed, as the bearded silhouette seemed to yawn and stretch. "What can I say? All this rain—it makes me sleepy. I'll tell you, I could really go for a Flat White about now. Two ristretto espresso shots, some whole milk steamed to perfection, a little ephemeral latte art right in the center. Sounds good, doesn't it?" He cocked his head in the near perfect silence. "No? What you want then, a bronson? At this hour? A good, earthy black IPA, perhaps? I could go for that. Something with a nice malty backbone—good for the old ticker." He laughed, seeming to think about it. "I know. Too conventional, right?" He shook his head. "Momma always said: she said, 'Atticus, all your taste is in your mouth.'"

There was a thin chuckle and a few clanks of the axe. "Kind of mean, don't you think? Anyway. That's what she said."

He began walking toward us—slowly, deliberately—dragging the handle, dragging its blade along the pavement.

"Look," I said. "We didn't come here looking for any ..."

"Any what?" He stopped about four feet in front of me, close enough at last for us to have a good look at him, and what we saw seemed utterly incongruous with what Roman had told us—except, of course, for the multitude of tattoos (mostly triangles), and even more so the washboarded scar, which ran from somewhere on his scalp and through an eye (over which one lens of his dark, plastic-framed glasses had been painted black) clear to his left shoulder. That much, at least, fit. What didn't fit was the slicked-back pompadour and long, full, meticulously-trimmed beard—Jesus, there was even product in it—nor, for that matter, the flannel lumberjack shirt and skinny jeans, not to mention the Converse sneakers. What didn't fit, as the similarly attired men holding laser-guided rifles emerged from behind overgrown automobiles and support columns, was that the feared and formidable Skidders were, when exposed to the light of day (and not to put too fine a point on it), *hipsters.*

"Well doesn't this just take the cake," said Lazaro, and spit.

"I take it we aren't what you expected," said Atticus. He leaned on the axe as though it were a cane. "I must say, neither are you." His good eye, which was a pale, piercing blue, dropped to our weapons. "You came well-armed. What are those—M4s? Not exactly an easy thing to come by—since Big Green fled the scene." He raised his chin and cocked his head, studying us. "And that helicopter. I mean, *damn.* What did you do? Raid a small airport? Got a pilot, even."

He began pacing, slowly, methodically. "That's better than a doctor. So, to summarize: You got a helicopter. You got military-issue rifles. You got, well, plumbing—I mean, you're clean, all of you. You even got ..." He stopped dead in his tracks, dead in front of Sam. "You even got—a girl!" He screwed up his face suddenly and leaned back, staring at Joan, who glowered at him. "Make that plural. Sorry. It's just that ..." He looked Sam up and down. "It isn't always this easy to tell—"

"Look, what do you want?" I snapped.

Atticus reared his head back as though he'd been wounded. "Jesus! Tone. I was just going to say how important it is for the fairer sex to be represented in any post-apocalyptic scenario. You know, women." He leaned close to me, I have no idea why. "My boys call them tassels—fuck if I know. Something out of Williamsburg, I suppose. Like putting crayons in your beard, or whatever." He stepped back to address us all. "All of which is just my way of saying—you have a home. A base. A place to hang your hat. And because of that, I've only got two questions." He hefted the axe suddenly and decisively—before switching it to his other hand and touching it to the ground. "Where? And why, since you have your own turf, would you come prancing onto ours—a crime punishable by death? I mean, just, holy bugfuck. It had to be for something good, right?"

"What's it matter if you're just going to kill us anyway?" protested Lazaro. "You said it yourself: 'a crime punishable by death.' So why should we tell you anything?"

"Because information is currency," said Atticus flatly. He added quickly: "One I might just accept in exchange for your lives. Along with your guns, of course. And maybe the girl. It really all depends on the quality of your—"

But I'd stopped listening: focusing instead on the darkness behind him, behind his men. Because something had moved there. Something amongst the cars.

Several somethings.

"The pharmacy," I interrupted quickly, almost breathlessly, "the one on Madison Street. B-Bartell Drugs. That's—that's where we were going." I looked sidelong at Sam as sweat beaded along my brow. "We were going to Bartell Drugs—for prenatal vitamins. I'm sorry, Sam."

"That's very interesting," said Atticus, matter-of-factly. "But considering we're on Marion, I'd say you overshot the mark."

I stared at Sam intensely, trying to communicate in secret, trying to communicate with my eyes alone. "We—couldn't get to it from there. There were raptors between us and it; at least, that's what I think they were. They—they were in some kind of utility tunnel, which was dark. I'm the only one who saw them. The others—they, they had to take my word. We we're looping around the building to bypass the tunnel when you opened fire." Sam faced forward again and squinted, her expression a mask, her composure unwavering. That's when *I* knew *she* knew.

"As for the guns—take them," I said, trying not to look into the dark. "Just let us get the supplements. Please."

I looked to find Atticus staring at me, his head at an angle, his mouth hanging open. Then he guffawed—once, twice—and paced away, raising the axe head as he did so, slapping the flat of its blade against his palm. *"Man.* You are one *noble* fuck. *All of you.* And here I thought you were just a bunch of hardened, cutthroat survivors—come to take a slice of our purloined pie, no doubt." He stopped suddenly and turned around. "You, with the wire-frame glasses. Raptor-spotter. What's your name, son?"

I glanced at Sam on one side and Nigel on the other.

"Jamie," I said, and looked at my shoes. "Jamie Klein."

"Jamie," he repeated, and approached to within a few feet. "Jamie Klein." He pinched the axe between his knees as he began to swing and stretch his arms. "Damn. That suits you, you know? I mean, you seem like a nice guy. A real mensch. Are you Jewish?"

I shook my head.

"No. Well, it's not important. What is important is that we establish a baseline. Something that, well, will get me the truth—when I ask a simple, goddamn question. So, I'm going to ask you one more time, before I give the word. Where is your base-camp? And why—you need to think about this, you might even say your life depends on it—have you come to Pioneer Square?"

"I told you," I said. "We needed medicine and supplements for—"

"The girl," he said, and took a step back—even as two of his men (who weren't training rifles) grabbed Sam by the upper arms and forced her to the pavement.

"Sorry about this, troops—I really am. But I did say it: You needed to think about this one. Carefully." He took up the axe and tapped its head on the pavement. "I mean, you don't get to be the Big Dog without keeping your word, right?" He raised the hatchet slowly, confidently, the leather of his half gloves crinkling. "And believe me when I say: When it comes to south Seattle, we *are* the Big Dog ..."

That's when something leapt up in the darkness and my eyes darted to the blur—in time to see a blue and red velociraptor pounce the farthest Skidder back: its sickle-foot claws latching firmly into his abdomen, its fore-talons gripping his broad, flannelled shoulders, its jaws closing about his head. And then all was screaming and gunfire—which lit up the garage like the fourth of July and thundered, cracking, off its walls—as I piledrived Atticus and wrested the axe from him; as everyone scrambled for their weapons and the raptors pounced upon more Skidders.

"Lazaro!" I remember yelling—knowing his shotgun could blow the gate, knowing he'd opened locked doors with it before—before a man screamed nearby and I looked: and saw his attacker biting off the top of his head—just opening it like a watermelon, taking everything but his long, full beard.

And then there was a shotgun blast and we were falling back, still firing at the velociraptors, still firing into Atticus' men—lighting up everything and everyone as we ducked beneath the gate and burst into the rain. As we hustled down Marion Street with Roman thundering above us and the screams of the Skidders still echoing in our heads.

Toward the Exchange Building and a gutted triceratops in the window of a Starbucks. Toward the research and development lab of Roman's former employer ... and something we knew only as *Gargantua*.

Someone needed to say something, anything. The danger in silence was that, post-Flashback, one inevitably heard the emptiness, the melancholy: the sound of the world just breathing in and out, dreaming. So, I said: "For her, the Flashback is over"—hoping it would break the spell of her liquefied eyes and deeply sunken sockets, the pale, wispy hair, the fuzzy white fungus in her nostrils and mouth. Hoping, I suppose, that it would drown out the Nothing—if only for a moment.

"No more power lunches for this babysan," said Lazaro, and spat. He kicked the spilt attaché case at the base of the cycad, where her feet should have been, and paper and cash swirled. "Here one minute—melded with a tree the next. Shit sucks."

Sam stepped closer, examining where the woman's face merged with the tree. "Initial Flashback, you think? Or an aftershock?"

I watched the rain—which had lessened to a drizzle— dribble down the corpse's face and neck. "I don't know, she seems pretty well preserved. Could have been an aftershock."

"Probably suffocated," said Nigel. "Tree manifested and her lungs couldn't expand. Jesus. What a horrible way to go."

I looked at Joan who was white as a ghost. "You all right?"

"Yeah. It's just that ..." She shook her head. "It's nothing."

She jumped as our walkie-talkies squawked; it sure looked like something to me. "Go ahead, Sea One," I said. "What's your twenty?"

I looked to see the Bell 206 arching over Elliott Bay.

"Just west of you—monitoring pack movements near the Colman ferry terminal. Carnotauruses, by the looks of it. I take it you're at the Exchange?"

"Affirmative—and awaiting instructions."

"Through the double doors, left at the first hall, all the way to the end. Austin Dynamics and Land Systems. They'll be a secure door—you'll have to blow it. And hurry, because there are predators of the human variety on the move in Pioneer Square."

I peered at the sky, at what Roman called the Mesozoic Borealis, watching the colors bleed in and out of each other, watching them shift and change shape. "Yeah, ah, about that. Requesting alternative escape route—Over. We have had contact with Skidders. I repeat, we have had contact with them. We— they're all dead. Over."

But there was nothing, just the sound of the helicopter.

At last Roman said, "That's unfortunate. But it doesn't change a thing. Escape route is still 1st Avenue through Pioneer Square to Edgar Martinez Drive—then I-90 to Issaquah. Do you copy?"

That's when I saw it: *him,* the kid, dirty-faced and wild-eyed, his hair like an unkempt mane, listening to us from the nearby stairwell—like the feral boy in *The Road Warrior,* I swear.

"Hey!" I shouted, drawing the attention of the others, "Hey, kid! Hold up!"

But he was already gone—climbing from the well at its opposite end, bolting up the shattered sidewalk like a gazelle. Weaving right at 2nd Avenue—where he vanished into the primordial mist.

"Jesus," said Lazaro, before the overheads had even finished flickering on. "I mean ... Who was this thing even built for, Godzilla?"

I stared at the vehicle, which was the length of a small yacht, say, 50 feet. "Well, not to put too fine a point on it, it was built for *us*. Or whoever survived whatever apocalypse Dannon had dreamed up."

I approached the rover and slid my hand up one of the tires—which was taller than I was, by about a foot. "Welcome to the world of big tech billionaires and their passion projects." The rubber felt stiff, unyielding, like polished wood. "His was to build a fully self-contained armored expedition vehicle—a kind of mini-Noah's Ark—something that could not only sustain life but go about exploring what was left of the world—if and when the shit ever hit the fan."

I circled the big rig while gazing up at its slanted cab and wide, black grill, its array of lights, its giant push and roll bars. The thing was like a van-version of the Cybertruck but on fucking steroids. "Reckon he was like Mr. Musk—in need of a challenge, but also a moral imperative to justify it. For him that was this apocalypse he saw coming." I paused to examine the roof turret and what appeared to be a .50-caliber machine gun. "A virus, maybe. Or a war. Dinosaurs probably weren't in his game plan."

"Looks they were getting ready to test it," said Sam. "Look."

I looked to where a massive steel ramp (we'd descended stairs to get to the production floor) ended at an equally massive door. "Good. Looks like this might be easier than we—"

There was a rattle of weapons followed by Lazaro shouting, "Stop! Get on the ground!" —and I hurried to see what the commotion was; at which instant I saw a man in a blue shop-coat standing by a huge sphere and holding what looked like a small, olive-colored ball over his head—a ball with a ring attached, through which he'd looped a trembling finger.

"He's got a bomb!" I shouted—but resisted raising my rifle. "Everyone just chill! Okay?"

No one did—chill, that is—but no one fired either, and a moment or two passed in silence.

At last, the man said, "See this big tank here, this round monstrosity?" He indicated the white metal container next to him, which was taller even than he was. "That would be propylene gas—enough to level this entire floor, maybe the building itself. See this?" He nodded at the olive-colored ball. "That's your standard military-issue hand grenade, courtesy of the kids who were stationed here before they *and* the city fell. See those?" He nodded at some handles and hoses near the floor. "Those are the valves I loosened as you were making your way here. If you don't smell it yet, you will. It's strong. Now. Any questions?"

"Only one," I said, and pushed up my glasses. "What do you want?"

He shifted his footing as though preparing for a long standoff. "I want you to lower your weapons," he said, and wiggled his fingers near the pin—keeping himself on his toes. "Lower them and kick them toward me, all of you. Then we'll talk."

Nobody said anything.

At last, I set down my rifle and motioned for the others to do the same. "Do it," I said, and slowly raised my arms. "You too, Lazaro. *Let's go.*"

The weapons clattered as they were placed on the floor and punted toward him.

He lowered his arms cautiously. "There, see? We're still capable of it—rational thought. It hasn't gone the way of the dinosaur." He laughed at that but kept the grenade close to his chest. "Yet."

He looked at our weapons as though running calculations through his head. "There's Neanderthals roaming the streets, did you know that? Real ones—not supporters of President Tucker." He paused, seeming to size us all up. "Remember them? With their little red hats and faces all puffed in rage?" He chuckled. "Fell off the flat earth, I guess. No, these are genuine *Homo sapiens neanderthalensis*—right beside modern man and triceratops; right beside honkers from the Jurassic and Cretaceous and Triassic. Just sort of one big medley—like Time itself was put in a blender, or a concrete mixer, or a cream separator, and churned."

He seemed to relax a little and even lowered the grenade.

"I'm Ewan, by the way. Ewan Homes. I—I was *Gargantua's* chief engineer. Before life put us all in the blender."

"Jamie," I said. "Jamie Klein. This is Sam." I indicated the others. "That's Lazaro, Nigel, and Joan. We—we're from Issa—"

"Jamie, don't," interrupted Sam.

"It's all right," I said—and meant it. I trusted him; I don't know why. "We're from Issaquah. Got a camp there in what used to be a drive-in theater; it's got walls, vegetable gardens, some chickens and goats—there's even some generators, if you want to watch a movie. The thing is—Ewan—it's not overcrowded. And what I'm going to suggest just now is that—"

"Nothing leaves this facility," he snapped—simply, with finality. "That includes me." He raised the grenade tentatively and reached for the pin—then hesitated, his eyes searching mine, or seeming to. "No ... no, I don't hear it. It's not there." He lowered the olive-colored explosive slowly, tentatively. "The guile of the predator, the cunning of the fox. It's not there. You speak ... earnestly."

I let down my arms carefully, incrementally, maintaining eye contact. "I speak as someone who has sought *Gargantua* while not knowing it had a guardian, a sentinel, who is yourself, or at least how you see yourself. I speak as someone who has faced the Big Empty alone just as you have—and knows it is not for lack of bread that a man dies, but lack of purpose, and that you have found yours in the guarding of this machine, this vehicle—a vehicle that, for whatever reason, you cannot even drive yourself, or you would have done so already. And I'll offer you another way—Ewan, chief engineer at Austin Dynamics and Land Systems, whose budget was 8.5 million per fiscal year and who's assistant was named Roman Daystrom, your best friend—if you'll just turn off that fucking gas."

By the time I'd reintroduced Roman and Ewan via radio, and the former had convinced the latter to not only come with us but to let someone other than himself drive *Gargantua* (Ewan, we were told, was blind as a bat), and Nigel had escorted the engineer to his quarters so he could retrieve some of his effects, the clock on the wall of the shop read half past one—more than enough time for the Skidders to have organized some type of counter-strike; a fact that weighed heavily on my mind as the women and I began gathering up specs and schematics and Lazaro paced the room impatiently.

"What the hell's taking them so long? You heard Roman— carnotauruses, heading this way. Oh, I forgot. Nigel's on Jamaican Time."

"They have been gone awhile," said Sam. "Maybe we should—"

"It's no good splitting us up," I said. "There's no telling how quickly we might have to leave. Nigel's got it—everyone just chill." I looked at Lazaro. "Can you give us a hand with these? They're going to be heavy."

"Why the hell are we carting them along, then?" He snatched up one of the boxes with a huff and headed for *Gargantua.* "Or him, for that matter? Dude is definitely a few sandwiches short of a picnic."

"You going to fix this thing when it—" began Joan, but Lazaro was already up the ramp.

We continued working in silence.

At length Sam said, "Who was he, you think? That kid?"

I shrugged my shoulders. "Just a kid. Probably been on his own since the Flashback, who knows?" I heaped some manuals into a box—which created a cloud of dust. "He gave me a start, that's for sure. I didn't really get a good look at him."

"I did ..." She paused as though visualizing him. "He had bones around his neck, did you know that? Or teeth—like, really big ones. He'd strung them together as a sort of necklace. Isn't that odd, you think?"

Our faces were close as I stopped to reflect. "I don't know. Is it? Maybe he's extracting them from dead Barneys, like trophies. I confess, my first thought was that he'd gone feral. And yet ... He was wearing contemporary clothes, I remember that. Puffy coat, jeans, tennis shoes. I mean, he wasn't like Mowgli or anything."

She looked at me and started to grin. "I didn't think he was like *Mowgli* ..."

"All right! Drop your cocks and grab your socks," belted Lazaro—from the top of the ramp. "They're back."

I looked to see Nigel and Ewan entering the shop from the left, the latter seeming like an utterly new man—his hair no longer mussed; his clothes no longer a catastrophic mess.

"Apologies, apologies, a thousand apologies," he said, before pausing to admire *Gargantua.* "But a maiden voyage such as this requires a fresh change of clothes." He looked on a moment longer and then dropped to one knee—began ruffling through his overpacked bags. "Ah, yes, here it is. It's—I opened it with Nigel." He withdrew a corked bottle—which glinted darkly in the light from a high window. *"Voila!* One of eight bottles of Dom Perignon Rose champagne, Vintage 1959, served in Persepolis in 1971 by the then-Shaw of Iran."

He looked at us with a face flushed with excitement, and we looked back.

"To—to celebrate the 2500th anniversary of the founding of the Persian Empire ... by Cyrus the Great." Disappointment stole over his face like a shadow. "It's—it's to break over the bow, as it were. To christen *Gargantua."* Nobody said anything.

"Yeah—well. Waste of liquor, anyway. Especially when I've got so much celebrating to do. I'll, ah—I'll just get the door. Over there."

He moved up the ramp toward the garage door.

That's when I thought of Lazaro's admonition, I don't know why: *You heard Roman—carnotauruses, heading this way.*

"Wait, Ewan," I said.

But he was already there, triggering the great door with his fist, turning to look at us as it rattled upward, pulling the cork from the champagne. "Life is for the living," he said, and toasted us with the bottle. "And this stuff ..." He poured champagne into his mouth and down the sides, soaking his clean, white shirt, splattering the floor with foam. "This is for howl—"

But then the door was open, and they were there, the carnotauruses, and one closed its jaws about his scalp while another laid wide his abdomen (and another took up his legs) so that, howling, he was opened like a pizza being groped by eager hands. And then they themselves howled and piled over his body, and all we could do was to run—everyone save Nigel, who had his trimmer, which he started with a sputter—because our weapons were already in the rover.

Would we have made it to the truck if Nigel hadn't done what he did? I don't know—maybe. But I doubt it. The fact is these carnotauruses were *moving*—faster than I'd ever seen them move before—and had cut the distance between us in half before I heard the revving of Nigel's trimmer and saw him sweeping it across a dinosaur's belly, opening it like a can of spaghetti.

"Someone start the truck!" he shouted, his voice raw, animalistic, "I'll hold them off as long as I can!"

I scrambled up the stairs after Sam and Joan but before Lazaro. "Joan, this is your gig," I said, before essentially falling through a portal into the cockpit. "Get us out of here."

But she just stood there, looking around the deck and the crush of dials and switches; looking as if the vehicle itself might swallow her at any moment. "No ... No, I'm sorry. But I can't ... I just ..."

I indicated the co-pilot's seat. "Sam."

She buckled into her harness as I took the driver's seat and did the same, hoping that what Roman had told me was true—that *Gargantua* could pilot herself—and hoping, too, that I could remember the test protocol he'd so wisely insisted I study.

"*Gargantua,* this is Jamie—and I'm going to be your test driver today." I looked out the massive, slanted windshield to where Nigel had thrust his trimmer's saw-head into the mouth of a carnotaurus, only horizontally, after which he leveraged the shaft brutally—and popped off the top of the thing's head. "We are go for power on. I repeat: We are go for power on. Initiate protocol."

I watched as blood geysered from the beast's lower mandible—even as nothing seemed to happen with the vehicle.

"*Gargantua.* Initiate protocol."

"I got a bad feeling about this," said Sam, even as the creatures closed in around Nigel, and Lazaro opened fire from the ramp. "I mean, if you could just bounce in here and say 'go' then it obviously—"

"Clearance is Delta-Delta—*Dawn,*" I said rapidly, recalling the code words Roman had insisted I memorize, recalling how well he'd prepared me should something happen to Joan, as the consoles lit up like Christmas trees and the screens flickered to blue life; as the rover's hybrid engines hummed and whirred and pulsed, powerfully. "Issaquah via I-90, *go!*"

And then we were moving, smoothly, robustly (after an initial lurch), as one of the screens showed the stairs beginning to retract and Nigel rushed onto them—where he was assisted by Lazaro—as we clanked onto the ramp and powered up its traction-metal and finally burst onto the street.

"Sea One, this is Away Team Alpha, we are on our way!"

I looked up through the cockpit's huge windshield in time to see the Bell 206 thundering overhead—zooming toward Pioneer Square and the headquarters of the Skidders; zooming toward Edgar Martinez Drive and I-90 and *home.* "Do you copy?"

"Copy you loud and clear, Away Team Alpha," said Roman at last, euphorically, and laughed. "Congratulations."

I looked over my shoulder as Nigel and Lazaro joined us on the bridge, then forward again through the tinted windshield—where the streetlights were passing dangerously close to the roof. "Everybody hang on, we could run out of clearance fast."

There was a *frap-frap-frap* as the twigs of trees started colliding with us. That's when I first noticed it: him, her—a lone figure—walking out into the middle of the road, stopping between us and Pioneer Square. Turning to face us as I instinctively hit the brakes.

"Auto-pilot disengaged," said a voice—Majel Barrett's from *Star Trek,* I swear; some geek's idea of a joke.

"Is that who I think—" Sam started to say but then trailed off.

I peered through the angled glass, which was bullet-proof, I presumed, I mean it was *thick,* as the truck ground to a stop and the figure came into focus—beard, flannel, and all.

It was Atticus.

"Well, well," said Lazaro, sardonically. "Slippery motherfucker, isn't he?" He added: "What's that?"

I looked to where another figure had entered the street to join him, a smaller figure, wearing a puffy black coat and blue jeans, whose hair was wild and unkempt. A figure who wore a necklace of large teeth around his neck—T. rex teeth, by the looks of it—and smiled gap-toothed as Atticus ruffled his hair.

The kid. The feral boy. Mowgli, whatever.

But that wasn't all, for there were others now too—not Skidders, there were no beards or flannel or Converse shoes— just people: men, women and children, most of them disheveled, who walked out single-file and formed a living fence across the road— even as another group (visible on one of the monitors) did the same behind us. And it was at precisely that instant that I glimpsed the first of the red dots—which were fleeting, erratic, sometimes holding on a person's head, sometimes roaming—and realized just how much trouble we were in. How trapped we'd become.

Time had stopped—not because of any Flashback or roiling time-storm or strange, vague lights in the sky, or because fully three quarters of the human population had vanished without a trace (and been replaced with prehistoric flora and fauna), but because we'd been outsmarted, pure and simple. And now all we could do was watch, as the rows of people in front of us and behind began to lay themselves on the ground and another brought Atticus a megaphone—which he lifted to his mouth while steadying himself with his ax and directed at the rover's cab.

"Well, just check ... this ... out! Damn!" He acted as though he might slap his knees. *"Gargantua One.'* What do you know? I mean, what will they think of next?"

The feral kid appeared to laugh as the wind gusted suddenly and the branches of the trees swayed.

"Those are *some* prenatal vitamins, I must say. I can see now why you thought this was important enough to risk your lives. Not to mention kill or allowed to be killed some of my best men."

My mind raced. Time. We needed time. I searched the banks of switches and readouts for a means of communication and found a toggle marked 'loudspeaker,' which I flipped.

"I seem to recall you were about to chop off Sam's head," I said, hoping it would keep him jabbering for at least a minute.

"And snip such a fine tassel?" He laughed. "Not on this watch, Midtown. You need to learn to recognize bullshit when you see it—"

I switched off the loudspeaker. "We need ideas—fast."

"For what?" said Nigel. "You can see all the red dots. He's got us in a hopeless situation, tactically."

"That's *bullshit,* man," snapped Lazaro. "There's a machine gun on top of this thing."

"And what are you going to shoot at? The air? They're hidden in the buildings all around. You'll be lucky to get in a burst before—"

"He's right," I said. "It's no good. Those people aren't just human barriers—they're hostages. We start fooling around with that gun ... and they're toast." I keyed the mic of my radio. "Sea One, this is Away Team Alpha. Come back."

Atticus continued: "... gangland theatrics. How else was I going to get you to talk? I knew you were after *some* kind of kale ..."

Our radios squawked. "Go ahead."

"Listen, Roman, quickly: We are surrounded by Skidders and need technical data regarding *Gargantua*— defense mechanisms, weapons systems, whatever you got. And we need it fast."

He responded almost instantly. "Where is Ewan, *asleep?*"

I started to speak but hesitated, wondering if I should tell him now or later; if I should disrupt his focus. "He ... he's passed out in the back. He was ... he was pretty drunk."

But there was no response and we listened to Atticus as we waited; luckily for us, the motherfucker liked to talk.

"... and consider yourselves lucky you didn't run into, say, Antifa. Don't laugh—those little fuckers are hard. Like a bunch of Viet Cong running around in black pajamas. Saw them go up against a militia once—might have been White Out, I'm not sure ..."

"Okay, listen up," came Roman at last, his voice full of urgency. "The gun up top can be operated from inside as well as out, you just have to use the joystick, which is on the right side of the driver's seat. There should be a pair of sighting goggles also, hanging above, which are slaved to the .50-cal—you'll use these to acquire targets. Just hit 'auto' on the joystick and you'll be golden. There's also smoke dispensers mounted on both sides of the vehicle, the switch is right above you, but I don't advise using them—they're too effective and you'll be blinded for several minutes. At least. Other than that, the vehicle was designed primarily for exploration, so I don't know what—can I provide any sort of air cover? Prop-wash, for example?"

"Negative, I repeat, negative. It's too tight in here. Just stand by."

Atticus, meanwhile, was still going on: "... ever seen a pack of allosaurs take down a diplodocus? That's what this was like. Just hit and run, hit and run, until the big dumb bastards collapsed from their own weight. Now they're dead—and a bunch of skinny anarchists have AR-15s ..."

I peered at the old buildings through the trees and at the darkened windows, many of them without glass. If it had been even slightly foggy or misty—as it had been earlier—we might have traced the beams right back—

My heart must have skipped a beat, I'm sure of it. *Jesus,* I thought. *Could it be that simple?*

"What is it?" asked Sam, sounding concerned.

I reached for the goggles and slowly slid them on, then gripped the joystick cautiously. "See that switch right there? The illuminated blue one?" She nodded warily, her face pale. "That's the smoke dispensers. When I give the word, I want you to flip it, okay? Don't be scared."

"What are you doing?" snapped Lazaro, with a clear edge to his voice. "Sandahl, what is he doing?"

"I'm getting ready to target those snipers," I said, and pressed the 'auto' switch, making sure to keep my head perfectly still lest the machine gun swivel and alert Atticus. "Nigel, get ready on the loudspeaker. On my word only I want you to order those people to get up and get clear. Make sure they understand—we are coming through. There can be no confusion. Lazaro, I want you to open the side door—but do not lower the ramp—and take a position; at my word you'll use my M4 to clear targets on the *right* side of the truck only, understand? I'll take care of the left and then swing around to help you."

I waited for him to acknowledge and when he didn't, I snapped, "Do you understand? We don't have time for this."

"Yes, I understand!"

"Good. Now—Joan. Where are you, girl?"

She stirred in the seat behind me. "I'm—I'm sorry, Jaime. I'm so sorry. But I—"

"You don't have to be," I said. "I know it's cramped in here. And I'm sorry I didn't listen to you when you tried to tell me about ... your condition. But you're going to make it, all right? We all are. Just buckle up, hold tight, and try to focus on what's outside. Just like you did in the helicopter, okay? You got this."

"I got this," she repeated, and exhaled sharply.

Atticus, meanwhile, had been counting down. "Three ... two ... *one.*" He sighed and lowered the megaphone—then lifted it to his mouth again. "The problem with you, Jaime, is that you just—don't—listen. Now I just explained to you what was going to happen if I reached 'one' and you hadn't come out, and *goddamned* if you didn't come out. So. What's going to happen now is that we're going to kill one of these people for every 30 seconds you remain inside the vehicle—starting immediately." He directed the bullhorn at the upper floors of one of the buildings. "Hershel? You awake up there?"

"Get ready," I said.

"I'm awake," came a voice, though it was impossible to tell exactly where from.

"Fine," said Atticus. "Hershel, in 30 seconds, I want you to place your site on the head of ... that little girl, right there." He gestured at a storefront on our right side—Simply Seattle. "Green coat, last one on the end, right next to the display window. Copy that there, Chief?"

The man didn't hesitate. "Twenty-nine! 28! 27 ..."

I toggled the loudspeaker myself. "We're coming out," I said, suddenly, and glanced at Sam. "We're trying to figure out how."

There was a silence as Atticus seemed to think about this.

At last, he said, "Well, how complicated could it be? Just open the door. Hershel, keep counting ..."

"Twenty-three, 22, 21 ..."

"It's not that simple," I hurried to say, "It's, like, pressurized or something." To the others I said, "On my mark, okay? Get ready."

"We're at 18 seconds and counting, James," said Atticus. "Best clean your glasses and get with it."

"Seventeen, 16, 15 ..."

"Okay! Okay. We're depressurizing. Right ... *now.*"

And then Sam was toggling the smoke as I gripped the joystick tightly and Nigel took over the loudspeaker and Lazaro opened the side door, after which we cursed loudly and bent to our tasks, and, together, threw wide the gates of Hell.

It started, innocuously enough, with the *thump, thump, thump* of the smoke grenades, which launched at an angle from both sides of the cab and bounced off the overhanging tree branches—as well as breaking at least one nearby window— before falling to the pavement and bursting into clouds of gray smoke. Nor did anything happen immediately—as if everyone outside were in a state of shock. But then the smoke began to rise, obscuring everything, and illuminating too the beams of the lasers—which lengthened as I tracked them and led straight to the top floors of Doc Maynard's Public House—at which I depressed the 'fire' button and lit them up; even as Lazaro opened fire on the other side and feedback whined from the loudspeakers.

"Move—if you would live," shouted Nigel. "Get up and run, all of you! We're advancing."

But we'd spent our surprise and what Skidders remained in the windows rallied, opening fire indiscriminately, shooting blindly into the smoke, as their muzzles flashed like Xs, and we continued to cut them down; as Nigel repeated his directive and my foot hovered over the gas. "Are they clear yet, Sam? Are they out of the way?"

I continued to fire even as bullets impacted the windshield and side window, cracking them in rings, leaving huge craters.

"I don't know, I think so," she said. "They're scrambling, I saw that much."

"Then we're going," I said. "Nigel, give them a final warning."

"But how can you drive with the windows smashed?" protested Sam—even as more rounds impacted the glass. "How can—"

"Engage the auto-pilot!" I shouted, aiming at what appeared to be the last holdout, holding down the 'fire' button, feeling the cab vibrate and shake.

"But I don't know—"

"Got it," blurted Joan—having rallied herself, or so it seemed.

And then the engines were humming, pulsing—winding up like great turbines, moving us forward into the mists.

"We're all clear!" shouted Lazaro. "It's Issaquah or bust!"

And with that we emerged from the clouds; to see what could only be Atticus himself running down 1st Avenue, his unbuttoned flannel shirt flying out behind him, his Converse sneakers pounding the pavement. The feral kid, meanwhile, was nowhere to be seen.

"Jesus, does he even know we're coming?" asked Sam.

"No," I said, squinting between the cracks. "We're on electric."

"Good," said Lazaro. "Run the fucker over."

I tapped the gas pedal, to take it out of auto-pilot, having found a spot through which I could see clearly. "I'm reverting to manual," I said, having no intention of running him down like a dog.

But nothing seemed to happen; we just continued moving forward—picking up speed—until trees were blowing past on one side and buildings were blurring past on the other.

"It'll go around," said Joan. "The sensors haven't picked him up yet, that's all."

But I wasn't so sure as the gap between us closed rapidly—so rapidly I could see his buttocks pumping beneath the skinny jeans and his keys dancing wildly at his hip. And then he disappeared beneath the rig with a pronounced *thump* and the cab jolted, bouncing once, and I glanced at the rear-view monitor in time to see a skid of dark blood and bone and guts extending out behind us almost indefinitely.

"Okay ... so I thought I was better," said Joan, still staring at the screen—her face green as a ghost. "But I'm not." Her cheeks puffed suddenly as though she might vomit. "We need to pull over, I think. Like, *now.*"

"Okay. I'll try," I said, and tapped the gas pedal.

But this time, control reverted back to me—as it was supposed to do—and as we passed Jackson Street, I began looking for a place to pull over, because it was finished, I knew. We were safe.

We'd survived the Dinosaur Apocalypse. Again.

By the time we did pull over—or rather, ground to a halt in the middle of the street—rain was starting to speckle the windshield (or what was left of it) and the sky had darkened, none of which prevented Joan from leaping onto her seat the moment we stopped and grabbing the handle of one of the ceiling hatches.

"Is that a good idea?" I asked, as she turned the handle and pushed the hatch open. "We haven't even had a look around yet—"

But she had already burst through the opening and was gasping for air, sucking it into her lungs in great, shuddering gulps, exhaling as though she'd been holding her breath for a lifetime. "I—I don't care," she rasped, as though she were collapsing from exhaustion. "Couldn't ... couldn't breathe. Couldn't—do it a second longer."

"What's wrong with her?" asked Lazaro.

"She's fine," I said, breathing in the fresh air myself, feeling relieved, almost euphoric. "Little bit of claustrophobia, that's all. Take all the time you need, Joan. We're done with this now. We're all done."

Everybody seemed to relax in their seats, exhaling, stretching their muscles. It was the first real rest we'd had since leaving the drive-in that morning.

"Well, would you look at that," said Lazaro at last, peering out his window, and laughed.

I followed his gaze to where a black awning with white letters read COWGIRLS INC – AMERICAN SALOON.

"Never heard of it," I said, and winked at Sam.

"I could go for a drink or five about now," said Joan, and laid her head on her arms.

"I could go for one of those waitresses dancing on the bar and shaking her ass in my face," said Lazaro.

"Ewan had the right idea," sighed Joan, and shifted her weight. "With that bottle of champagne, I mean." She fell silent for a moment as though remembering. "What was he saying when ... when ..."

I thought back on it, on that awful moment when the carnotauruses had torn him limb from limb. "He was in the middle of saying 'howl,' I think," I said, and slumped against my window. "That the champagne was for howling, not busting over *Gargantua,* to christen it. I think he'd been alone so long that he'd died a little, or even a lot. We'd given him hope. A reason to howl at the moon, or something."

Nobody said anything as the clouds rumbled overhead and the rain grew heavier, drizzling around the ringed cracks in the windshield, trickling down Joan's coveralls.

"I want to dance in the rain," said Sam, softly.

"We want you to too," said Lazaro.

"Aaoooh!" crooned Joan, and when I looked, she'd stood straight again and spread her arms at the sky.

"Aaoooh!" responded Lazaro, almost as though he were drunk.

And then Nigel joined in, followed by Sam, and finally myself, and there we all were, howling at the sky like a bunch of damn lunatics, beating our chests for having survived another day—spreading our fiery, Phoenix wings in defiance of what we'd done and still had to do and what had become of the world.

And it was on the tip of my tongue to suggest we actually go in and have a drink—or five—when Joan's body seized up like a vice and her voice became muffled, at which I squinted through Lazaro's window and saw the lower body of the tyrannosaur (or whatever it was), and realized its head would have been exactly where she was—and that the new sound I was hearing, which was a garbled sound, an obscene sound, was that of Joan screaming; whimpering; suffocating no doubt in the monstrous animal's palette, before it jerked its head and she was yanked clean from the hatch. Before the great and terrible animal stepped back and began shaking her like a ragdoll, even though she was surely dead already, hurling her against the pavement with a sickening *smack,* pinning her there with its tri-clawed foot; which is when I stepped on the gas—but not before seeing her come apart like mozzarella—and drove away as fast as I could.

After which we drove the rest of the way home in silence and tried not to think of all the blood splattered around the hatch and pooled like thick, dark wine in her seat. After which we kept our heads down and our eyes alert, all the way to Issaquah and the drive-in we called home. All the way until we greeted Roman at the heli-pad with open arms and walked together, through the cool shadows of the carports, to our respective campers and trailers and RVs.

CONTRIBUTORS

Wayne Kyle Spitzer is an American writer, illustrator, and filmmaker. He is the author of countless books, stories and other works, including a film (*Shadows in the Garden*), a screenplay (*Algernon Blackwood's The Willows*), and a memoir (*X-Ray Rider*). His work has appeared in *MetaStellar—Speculative fiction and beyond, subTerrain Magazine: Strong Words for a Polite Nation* and *Columbia: The Magazine of Northwest History*, among others. He holds a Master of Fine Arts degree from Eastern Washington University, a B.A. from Gonzaga University, and an A.A.S. from Spokane Falls Community College. His recent fiction includes *The Man/Woman War* cycle of stories as well as the *Dinosaur Apocalypse Saga*. He lives with his sweetheart Ngoc Trinh Ho in the Spokane Valley.

E.M. Anderson (she/her) is a queer, neurodivergent writer working in the College of Arts & Sciences at Lourdes University. She has short stories forthcoming in GutSlut Press's anthology *Suicidaliens* and SJ Whitby's anthology *Awakenings* in 2022. Her poetry has appeared in *Wizards in Space Literary Magazine.* It is her doom to one day vanish in the depths of a forest, never to be seen again, after ignoring the repeated warnings of the locals to stay out of the woods. Until that fateful day, you can find her on Twitter at @elizmanderson.

Mary Jo Rabe grew up on a farm in eastern Iowa, got degrees from Michigan State University and the University of Wisconsin-Milwaukee. She worked in the library of the Archdiocese of Freiburg, Germany, for 41 years and retired to Titisee-Neustadt, Germany. She has published "Blue Sunset", inspired by Spoon River

Anthology and The Martian Chronicles, electronically and has been published in Pulphouse, Fiction River, Penumbric Speculative Fiction, Alien Dimensions, Fabula Argentea, The Lost Librarian's Grave, and other magazines and anthologies.

Blog: https://maryjorabe.wordpress.com/

She indulges in sporadic Facebook and Twitter activity, facebook.com/rabemj and @maryjorabe

Anthony Ferguson is an author and editor living in Perth, Australia. He has published over sixty short stories and non-fiction articles in Australia, Britain, and the United States. He wrote the novel *Protégé,* the non-fiction books, *The Sex Doll: A History,* and *Murder Down Under,* edited the short-story collection *Devil Dolls and Duplicates in Australian Horror* and coedited the award-nominated *Midnight Echo #12.* He is a committee member of the Australasian Horror Writers Association (AHWA), and a submissions editor for Andromeda Spaceways Magazine (ASM). He won the Australian Shadows Award for Short Fiction in 2020.

Laurence Klavan wrote the story collection, "'The Family Unit' and Other Fantasies," published by Chizine. An Edgar Award-winner, he received two Drama Desk nominations for the book and lyrics of "Bed and Sofa," the musical produced by the Vineyard Theater in New York and the Finborough Theatre in London. His website is www.laurenceklavan.com.

Riley Winchester is a writer from Michigan.

Terry Sanville lives in San Luis Obispo, California with his artist-poet wife (his in-house editor) and two plump cats (his in-house critics). He writes full time, producing short stories, essays, and novels. His short stories have been accepted more than 460 times by journals, magazines, and anthologies including The Potomac Review, The Bryant Literary Review, and Shenandoah. He was nominated twice for Pushcart Prizes and once for inclusion in Best of the Net anthology. Terry is a retired urban planner and an accomplished jazz and blues guitarist - who once played with a symphony orchestra backing up jazz legend George Shearing.

Sam Finn was a terrific ER doc in a scary, busy ER for 25 years. He brings his love of cold, hard grit and compassion for those less fortunate souls—in this cold, hard society of ours—to his writing. He's paid his dues, is happily retired, self-published a medical thriller, Heartbeat (available online), and now writes sci-fi.

Gregg Sapp is a Pinnacle Award winner and Pushcart Prize nominated author of the "Holidazed" series of satires, each of which is centered around a different holiday. To date, there are four books in the series: "Halloween from the Other Side," "The Christmas Donut Revolution," "Upside Down Independence Day," and the latest, "Murder by Valentine Candy." Previous books include "Dollarapalooza," set in a dollar store, and "Fresh News Straight from Heaven," which is based on the folklore of Johnny Appleseed.

Charles Wilkinson's publications include *The Pain Tree and Other Stories* (London Magazine Editions, 2000). His stories have appeared in *Best Short Stories 1990* (Heinemann), *Best English Short Stories 2* (W.W. Norton, USA), *Best British Short Stories 2015* (Salt), *Confingo, London Magazine* and in genre magazines/ anthologies such as *Black Static, The Dark Lane Anthology, Supernatural Tales, Theaker's Quarterly Fiction, Phantom Drift* (USA*), Bourbon Penn* (USA), *Shadows & Tall Trees* (Canada), *Nightscript* (USA) and *Best Weird Fiction 2015* (Undertow Books, Canada). His anthologies of strange tales and weird fiction, *A Twist in the Eye* (2016), *Splendid in Ash* (2018) and *Mills of Silence* (2021) appeared from Egaeus Press. A full-length collection of his poetry came out from Eyewear in 2019. Eibonvale Press l published his chapbook of weird stories, *The January Estate,* in 2022. He lives in Wales. More information can be found at his website charleswilkinsonauthor.com.